FOR THE LAST TIME: Welcome to Yawnee Valley!

Or, if you've never read a book in this series before, for the first time: Welcome to Yawnee Valley!

Yawnee Valley is full of hills, and Yawnee Valley is full of cows. The hills are green. The cows are various colors. Mostly the cows are black and white, but there are quite a few brown ones. Bob Barkin, a prominent local farmer, claims to own a blue cow, but other people say she is really just grayish. Here is a picture of the cow in question:

We realize this picture, rendered only in black ink, will not help you decide for yourself whether Bob's cow is blue. Sadly, we cannot afford to print these books in color. Still, we hope you enjoyed the illustration. That's a very good-looking cow!

Yawnee Valley was almost known as "The Milky Pearl in America's Dairy Diadem," a motto rejected by the Yawnee Valley Council because only one member knew what a diadem was. (It's a crown.) The town is home to more cows than people—which you would know if you lived there, which you probably do not, because not many people do, and cows cannot read books. Many billions of people live on Earth, and only 9,980 of them live in Yawnee Valley.

So:

What are the odds that this little town would be home to not one but two world-class pranksters?

And what are the chances that two of Earth's billions of people should meet in Yawnee Valley and discover that they were soul matches, boon companions, true amigos, and best friends?

What is the probability that this sleepy hamlet should serve, even briefly, as the stage for one of history's great pranking duos, a pair of notorious practical jokers known as the Terrible Two?

We don't know the answers to these questions. Math was never our best subject. But the odds are long! The chances are slim! It seems very unlikely!

And yet.

Yawnee Valley is the hometown of Miles Murphy and Niles Sparks. Here they are now:

Wait. Sorry. That looks wrong. You can only see Niles in that picture. That is because they are in the middle of a prank. Here is a picture from five minutes earlier:

Much better. Here we go.

IT **WAS SUNDAY.** It was autumn. Miles and Niles, wearing very large coats, sat side by side near the back of the number three bus. The three ran by Niles's house on Buttercream Lane, out past a pasture owned by Bob Barkin, which is where they were headed. Normally, they would have just ridden their bikes, but today they were carrying a bunch of stuff.

Beneath their coats, between the two of them, Miles and Niles had strapped to their bodies:

- Three cans of livestock paint, deep purple
- Three cans of livestock paint, neon green
- One cardboard stencil made from a refrigerator box, polka-dot pattern
- A really long measuring tape
- Pruning shears
- Hand tools wrapped in a leather carrying case
- A Brünte 3030 Hand Reel Push Lawn Mower, disassembled.

"Are you sure this paint will stick to its fur?" Miles asked.

"Yes," Niles said.

"But are you sure sure?" Miles asked.

"Yes yes," Niles said. "It's livestock paint. That's what it's for."

"Oh," said Miles. "OK."

Miles didn't know much about livestock paint, or livestock, because he hadn't grown up around cows. He had grown up a thousand miles away, in an apartment in a pink building that was close to the ocean. Two years ago, Miles and his mom had moved to Yawnee Valley. And even though it had only been two years, Miles felt like everything that had happened back then, back there in that town by the sea, had happened to somebody else. It felt like his real life was the stuff that had happened *since*. For Miles, it was like his story began when he met Niles Sparks, which is what it can feel like when you meet your best friend.

"I thought we were going to wear sunglasses," said Niles, who was wearing sunglasses.

"Oh yeah," said Miles. He got his sunglasses out of his coat and put them on.

"Why are we wearing sunglasses?" he asked.

Niles shrugged. "Big coats. Sunglasses. It seemed like a cool look."

Miles admired their reflection in the window.

"Yeah," he said. "It sure is."

The bus stopped at a corner. Its doors hissed open and a woman in a cap and a navy blue uniform stepped aboard.

"Tickets," she said to an old man in the front row.

The old man pulled out a bus ticket. She promptly punched it—click click!—and handed his ticket back.

"Thank you," said the old man kindly.

The bus woman moved on without saying "you're welcome."

"Tickets."

A little girl in the next row handed over two tickets, one for her and one for her mother.

"My mom said I could hold our tickets!" said the little girl.

"She didn't want to pay for them though!" said her mother.

The little girl laughed.

Her mother laughed.

The bus woman did not laugh.

She did not even smile.

She just punched the tickets—click click!—and handed them back.

"That lady is a mean person," the little girl whispered.

"She might just be having a bad day," said her mother.

The little girl's mother was right. The bus woman was having a bad day. That morning, a veterinarian had told her that her cat, Joseph, was "on the chubby side." Then, five minutes ago, her husband, whose name was also Joseph, had texted her that the store was out of paprika, which was unacceptable, because on Sunday nights the bus woman always made goulash. All week she looked forward to goulash. It was her second-favorite thing in the world. So yes, she was having a bad day.

But to be fair, the little girl was also right. The bus woman was a mean person. Even on good days she was like this: grim, unfriendly, perfunctorily punching tickets. Her favorite thing in the world, even above goulash, was throwing people off the bus.

Not *literally* throwing them, of course.

Ejecting them.

Although at night, sometimes the bus woman would smile in her sleep as she dreamed of hurling passengers through the air—old men, little girls, and mothers somersaulting over lanes of traffic and tumbling through the tall grass that grew by the side of the road.

So yes, she was a mean person.

"Tickets," said the bus woman to a man who was already holding out his ticket.

In the back of the bus, Niles reached into the breast pocket of his coat.

His whole body tensed.

"What's wrong?" Miles asked.

Niles dug around in the pocket.

Then he dug around in all the coat's other pockets.

Then he stood up and checked the pockets of his pants.

"Niles, what's wrong?" Miles asked.

Niles shook his head and checked all his pockets again.

"Niles," said Miles.

"Miles," said Niles. He removed a single piece of paper from his breast pocket. "We only have one ticket."

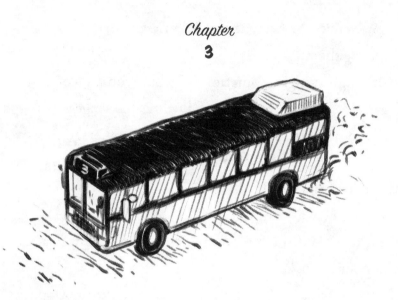

"WHAT DO YOU MEAN *we* only have one ticket?" said Miles.

"How many tickets do you have?" said Niles.

"None!" said Miles.

"Exactly," said Niles.

"But you said you were going to buy tickets for both of us," said Miles.

"I did!" said Niles.

"So why do you only have one?"

"I must have lost yours."

"Mine! Why is the lost one mine?"

"What?"

"Maybe you lost *yours*," said Miles. "Maybe that's *my* ticket."

"Tickets," said the bus woman to a kid wearing headphones.

"It doesn't matter whose ticket this is," said Niles, who was holding the ticket where Miles couldn't reach it. "We both need to get to Bob Barkin's farm or Operation: First Contact is a bust. This is a two-man job. Plus we're each carrying half a lawn mower. We need two tickets."

"OK." Miles stopped grabbing at the ticket. "So what do we do?"

Niles put the ticket back in his pocket. "We think."

They sat and they thought while the bus woman worked her way toward the back of the bus.

"Tickets."

Click click!

"Tickets."

Click click!

"She looks mean," said Miles.

"Yeah," said Niles.

"Tickets."

Click click!

"Got anything?" said Niles.

"No," said Miles. "You?"

"No," said Niles. "But we're kind of counting on you here."

"Me?" said Miles. "Why me?"

"Because you're good under pressure!" said Niles. "That's your whole thing!"

"Oh please," said Miles.

He looked down at his shoes.

"What?" said Niles. "That's a compliment! You're good on your feet! You always get us out of tight spots!"

"Well that's a lot of pressure!" said Miles.

"Yeah," said Niles. "BUT YOU'RE GOOD UNDER PRESSURE!"

"Stop saying that!" said Miles.

The bus woman had made it halfway to the boys.

"Tickets."

Click click!

"Tickets."

Click click!

Miles's head snapped up.

"I've got it," he said. "I'll hide."

"What?" said Niles.

Miles was slumped down in his seat, shrugging off his coat. "I'll hide," he said. "Hide me."

"Brilliant."

Niles helped Miles take off his coat. Then Miles got down on the floor, crawled underneath the seats in front of him, and curled up as small as he could, which was not very small, mostly because of all the pranking materials attached to his body.

"Cover me," said Miles.

Niles gently arranged the coat on top of Miles.

"Don't move," said Niles.

"No duh," said Miles.

Niles took off his sunglasses and rested his feet on what was probably Miles's head.

Their timing was perfect.

"Tickets."

The bus woman looked down at Niles.

Niles smiled back up at the bus woman.

"One moment, please, ma'am."

Niles reached into his breast pocket and removed two bus tickets.

He handed them over.

"One is for me, and the other's for my friend."

"Your friend?" asked the bus woman.

"Yeah, my friend down here on the floor."

Niles reached down and lifted a corner of the coat.

"Hello," Miles said.

"Why is he wearing sunglasses?" the woman asked.

"Good question!" said Niles. "Miles, why are you wearing sunglasses?"

Miles shrugged. "It seemed like a cool look."

"There you have it!" said Niles.

Niles smiled.

Miles smiled.

The bus woman made this face:

Look! It's hard to say for sure, but there appears to be a hint of a smile!

Click click!

She punched the tickets and handed them back to Niles.

"Thank you!" he said.

He placed the tickets in his pocket and pulled the coat back over Miles's face.

"Thank you," said Miles, from underneath the coat.

"Thank you," said the woman, and she moved on.

The coat on the floor shook with laughter.

"It's really gross down here," Miles said.

Niles was laughing too.

"Yeah," he said. "It's the floor of a bus."

"You knew I was going to hide," said Miles. "You knew the whole time."

"Yeah," said Niles. "I knew."

Of course Niles had known, and Miles knew that Niles had known, and this knowledge made them laugh harder. They laughed till their stomachs ached, till the corners of their eyes were wet with tears.

A hand emerged from underneath the coat, a hand with two fingers raised in the air, just like this:

And Niles touched his fingertips to Miles's fingertips, and they laughed some more.

They laughed because they understood what all great pranksters do: A practical joke can be a hatpin in the balloon of tyranny, a firecracker in the chapel of mundanity, but it can also be a secret handshake between friends. A prank is sometimes a slap. It is sometimes a pop. But it is sometimes a hug. A prank played on a fellow prankster can be a message in code. It says: "Hello, friend. I know you."

Chapter 4

THE NEXT DAY was Monday. It was a school day.

But it was not just any Monday and not just any school day. The next day was the first day of a new year at Yawnee Valley Science and Letters Academy.

Before school, Niles waited for Miles in the same spot he always waited for Miles: next to a fire hydrant, in the only square on the sidewalk that didn't have any cracks. A few feet away, on the front lawn, a huge marquee read PRINCIPAL BARKIN SEZ: WELCOME BACK, BOVINES! LET'S MAKE THIS OUR BEST YEAR!!!

Niles kicked a pebble with a shiny black oxford, size 8½. (Longtime readers may have noticed his feet had grown one and a half sizes since the start of this series!) A line of cars curved through the school's parking lot. Drivers honked their horns and jockeyed for spaces next to the curb.

A blue sedan swung up and parked next to Niles. Miles Murphy stepped out.

"Bye, Mom," said Miles.

He shut the car door.

6

Judy Murphy rolled down a window.
"Bye, Miles," she said. "Hi, Niles!"

"Hello, Judy!" said Niles. "I like your haircut! It really flatters your face!"

"Thank you, Niles," said Judy. "I like your haircut too!"

Niles ran his hand across the top of his head. "Oh thanks!" he said. "It wasn't exactly my choice but I'm getting used to it!"

Judy gave him a thumbs-up. It was a reassuring gesture ruined by an alarming flurry of whistle blowing nearby.

The whistle belonged to Coach B., who had Morning Drop-Off Duty. He ran up to the Murphys' car, blowing his whistle and jabbing his thumb toward the exit.

Coach B. did not like wearing the bright orange reflective Drop-Off Duty vest. He found it embarrassing, and compensated by blowing his whistle even more than usual, which was really saying something. "Move on, ma'am!" he shouted. "You gotta move on!"

"OK, but please don't call me ma'am!" said Judy. She waved at Miles, and then at Niles, and then at Coach B., before putting on her blinker and pulling away.

Coach B. went off to blow his whistle at some more cars.

Miles joined Niles in their sidewalk square.

"So you decided to wear the suit," he said.

"Yeah," said Niles. "I decided to wear the suit."

If you haven't read the first three books in this series, you should know that the Terrible Two was not just a pranking club. For a long time, the Terrible Two had been an S.P.C. (a

Secret Pranking Club). The main reason the club had been a secret was that Niles Sparks believed that a prankster should never be a yak. In Niles's S.P.L. (Secret Pranking Language), a yak was somebody who bragged about being a prankster. And the problem with bragging about being a prankster was that then everybody *knew* you were a prankster: your mom, your dad, your sister, your brother. Your teacher, your principal. The mayor. The grocer. The butcher, the baker, the candlestick maker, if you knew a candlestick maker, which Niles Sparks didn't. Your Aunt Janine, if you had an aunt named Janine, which Niles Sparks did. When people knew you were a prankster, they watched you constantly, trying to divine what prank you were going to play next. That kind of scrutiny made for, in Niles's words, "suboptimal operating conditions." That's because a good prank is surprising, and you can't surprise someone who is expecting to be surprised. Plus, let's say you somehow managed to catch the world unawares with a brilliant practical joke. Once people recovered, they were probably going to hold you responsible. Once people knew you were a prankster, you were the permanent prime suspect.

And so Niles Sparks had created a secret identity for himself. Over years, at first accidentally and then on purpose, he'd developed a reputation as a kiss-up, a lickspittle, a goody-goody. He cleaned the class pet's cage. He reminded teachers when they forgot to collect homework. He wore a suit to school every day. It was the perfect cover. But somewhere along the line (toward the end of book two, actually), his cover had been blown. The Terrible Two had been exposed. And now everybody knew that Niles Sparks was not a rule-loving toady. He was a rule-breaking ruffian.

If you have read the first three books in this series, you already know all this. You could have skipped the last two paragraphs. But it's too late now. Sorry.

Anyway, now their S.P.C. was just a P.C. And now Niles Sparks was just Niles Sparks. In the weeks leading up to their first day of school, Niles had been asking himself (and sometimes Miles) a big question:

How do you be a prankster, with everyone watching you all the time?

Which grew into an even bigger question:

How do you be yourself, *with everyone watching you all the time?*

And of course that question soon morphed into the hugest question yet:

Who is Niles Sparks?

And then, inside Niles's brain, all these questions coalesced, gathering together like skittering bits of claw and fur into one monstrous, terrifying question:

What should I wear on the first day of school?

That is how it is with big questions. Instead of answers, they lead to more questions, which lead to more questions, questions on questions on questions, and soon nothing is certain, and the only thing that can make you feel better is tightening the knot of a striped silk tie.

"I think I just like suits," Niles told Miles, in their square on the sidewalk in front of their school.

"Yeah," said Miles. "You look good in suits!"

They crossed the lawn, past hedges and trees, past flag and flagpole, past gaggles of kids, up to the front steps leading into the building they knew so well.

"Well, here we go," said Miles. "One last time."

"Yeah," said Niles. "Yeah."

For this was not just a Monday, not just a school day, and not just the first day of a new year of school. Miles and Niles (and everyone else in their class) were graduating this year. Today was the first day of their last year at Yawnee Valley Science and Letters Academy.

IN THE HALLWAY, students streamed by Miles and Niles. Since it was a new school year, lots of kids had new stuff. New folders with pictures of athletes or puppies. New pencils in new cardboard boxes: unsharpened, with perfect unsmudged pink erasers poking out of their tops. Lots of new lunchboxes: new plastic ones with characters from new movies that had just come out over the summer, new old ones made of tin with characters from movies that came out years ago. Brightly colored lunchboxes with squishy sides that were supposed to keep your drink cold but just absorbed the smell of your banana. New notebooks, new sneakers. Lucky kids had new textbooks. They had to write NEW on the inside covers, on a chart labeled CONDITION. The years would go on, and the chart would get filled out, from NEW to GOOD to FAIR to POOR. And then: DISCARD. There were new backpacks, looking like they'd been ironed by professional dry cleaners. Someday, a day when there was homework in every subject, their zippers would break. Their leather bottoms would get covered in drawings, made with blue ballpoint pen during boring classes. Their insides would get grease spots from melted chocolate chips of half-eaten granola bars forgotten in pouches. But today those backpacks were new. There were even new kids, to replace the old kids who'd left last year and now went to new schools.

"Who are all these kids?" Holly Rash asked. She'd fallen into step alongside Miles and Niles without saying hello. "They're so small. Were we ever that small?"

Miles and Niles did not reply to her question. It was a rhetorical question, and they all knew the answer. Yes. They had all been that small. They had all felt that new. Miles had more than once, since he'd had to switch schools.

Holly smiled at people she knew. "Hi, Ellen! Hey, Scotty!" She carried her books under her arm. A pencil was stuck behind her left ear.

"Where's your backpack?" asked Niles.

"What backpack?" said Holly. "I swore them off."

"You swore off backpacks?" Miles asked. "What's wrong with backpacks?"

"I think they look silly. 'Only bring what you can carry under your arm.' That's my motto this year."

"Wow," said Miles. "OK." He rolled his eyes and tightened the straps of his backpack. He was not convinced.

They rounded the corner with the drinking fountains.

A kid saw them, mid-drink. He yanked up his head, wiped off his mouth, and ran to catch up.

"Hey, GUYS!" said the kid. "Stop ZOOMING! WAIT up!"

This kid was named Stuart. He was dragging a suitcase on wheels behind him.

"Do you guys like my NEW BAG?" Stuart asked. "It's HUGE!"

"Again," Miles said, "what's wrong with backpacks?"

"What do you mean AGAIN?" Stuart said.

"We were talking before you came up," Niles said.

"I'm not doing backpacks anymore," said Holly.

"Wow," said Stuart, "it's SO WEIRD coming in right in the MIDDLE of something. I'm like, 'WHAT are you TALKING ABOUT?'"

Stuart laughed at his own joke, which wasn't really a joke. The other three kids nodded and waited for him to stop laughing, which he did, eventually.

"Now," said Stuart, "WHAT was I TALKING ABOUT?"

"Backpacks," said Niles.

"Oh YEAH," said Stuart. "BACKPACKS are too SMALL. I can carry EVERY BOOK in this bag, plus all my BINDERS and FOLDERS!"

"Why would you do that?" Holly asked. They were all making their way toward Room 22.

"Yeah," said Miles. "We have lockers."

"BECAUSE," Stuart said. He paused for dramatic effect. "THIS year I am using my LOCKER to store SNACKS!"

"Snacks?" said Niles.

"SNACKS!" said Stuart. "My WHOLE LOCKER is FILLED with SNACKS! I'm calling it the SNACK ZONE."

"OK," said Holly.

"Huh," said Miles.

"Neat," said Niles.

The four of them reached their classroom and picked out seats next to each other.

"So if you get HUNGRY during the day, or just want some SNACKS, COME to the SNACK ZONE! It's like a FRIDGE in the MIDDLE of SCHOOL, except it's not COLD!"

"So a cupboard," Holly said.

"That's FUNNY!" said Stuart.

"It is?" Holly asked.

Apparently it was, because Stuart was laughing again.

Miles looked at Stuart laughing, at Holly raising her eyebrows, at Niles smiling. He smelled the smells of Room 22—pencil shavings, soil from the plants Ms. Shandy grew in colorful pots along the row of windows, wet chalkboard. (Ms. Shandy hated whiteboards, and she didn't just erase her chalkboard—she wiped it down with a damp cloth every morning.) "Wow," Miles said softly. He surprised himself: He'd missed school.

The morning bell rang.

Ms. Shandy smiled at the class. "Good morn—"

Josh Barkin slid through the door.

"Just in time, Ms. Shandy!" he said.

Ms. Shandy sighed.

Josh pointed at Miles. "That nimbus is in my seat."

"If you wanted that seat, Josh, you should have gotten here on time."

"I *was* on time, Ms. Shandy. I already said that. You know, you should really listen to your students. It's the sign of a great teacher. In fact, a lot of great teachers say it's the *students* who teach *them*."

"Uh-huh," said Ms. Shandy.

"Plus, student-teacher interaction is a category on your staff evaluation, and I'd hate to report any negative interactions to my dad, who fills out your staff evaluation."

"Josh," said Ms. Shandy, "it's a new year. Let's try not to repeat our past mistakes. Take a seat."

Josh smiled at his teacher. "Whatever you say, Ms. Shandy."

On his way to the back row, he hit Niles in the face with his backpack.

"Oh, sorry!" As he swung around to apologize to Niles, Josh hit Miles in the face with his backpack.

"Sorry again!" Josh said. "I'm so clumsy today!"

"Josh," said Ms. Shandy.

"Just saying hi to my buds!" Josh said loudly.

"You little nimbuses," he added quietly.

Miles smiled.

Yes, it was good to be back.

MS. SHANDY SMILED at the class again.

"Now that we have endured that little Barkin interruption, we can get started. Good morn—"

The intercom screeched.

"PLEASE EXCUSE THIS INTERRUPTION. THIS IS YOUR PRINCIPAL, PRINCIPAL BARKIN, WITH AN IMPORTANT ANNOUNCEMENT. THIS MESSAGE IS FOR MILES MURPHY AND NILES SPARKS: PLEASE REPORT TO THE PRINCIPAL'S OFFICE, WHICH IS MY OFFICE, IMMEDIATELY."

"OOOOOOOOOOOOOOOOOOOOH MAMAMA-MAMAMAMA," said Stuart, which is what Stuart said when somebody got in trouble.

"You heard the man, guys." Ms. Shandy gestured to the door. "Now, good morn—"

"AND *THIS* MESSAGE IS TO THE REST OF YOU

STUDENTS, THE ONES WHO AREN'T MILES AND NILES: LET'S MAKE THIS OUR BEST YEAR! THANK YOU. END OF ANNOUNCEMENT."

This time Ms. Shandy waited five seconds before smiling.

"Good morn—"

"HOW DO YOU TURN THIS THING OFF?"

MILES AND NILES found themselves in a place many pranksters find themselves: the principal's office.

Specifically, Miles and Niles found themselves in this principal's office:

This principal's name was Principal Barkin. One wall of his office was covered with portraits of other principals, whose names were also Principal Barkin.

Principal Barkin came from a long line of principals. You could say being a principal was the Barkin family business, but if you did, a Barkin would correct you and say it was the family *calling*.

Miles and Niles took their regular seats: two small chairs on one side of Principal Barkin's big oak desk. On the other side, the principal side, the *power* side, sat Principal Barkin. He reclined in a plush leather chair, reading the newspaper.

"Well, boys, have you heard?" he said.

His chair squeaked as he leaned forward.

"The squeaking?" Miles asked.

Barkin's face flushed a faint purple. "No, Miles, not the squeaking. We have all heard the squeaking, which Gus was supposed to fix over the summer. Excuse me one moment."

He opened a notebook embossed with THE PRODUC-
TIVE PRINCIPAL in gold letters and added "TALK TO GUS
ABOUT SQUEAKING" to a long list labeled PROJECTS.
"Now." Principal Barkin slid his newspaper across the
table. "Have you heard the news?

Yawnee Valley Gazette

VOLUME CLXV, NO. VIII   PRICE $2.50

A COW OF A
DIFFERENT COLOR

Handsome Local Farmer
Makes First Contact Probabl

BY MARTHA STATHERS-SEYERS

"Some guys have all the luck," said Principal Barkin. "First he gets a blue cow, which if I'm being honest is really more grayish, and now this! This!"

He tapped his index finger on the photo that accompanied the article.

"That cow also looks grayish," said Miles.

"Well, yes, of course it does, Miles. It's a newspaper. They can't afford to print in color. But if you'd read the article before speaking, you'd know that this cow is bright green! With purple spots!"

Below Principal Barkin's desk, where he could not see, the Terrible Two exchanged a secret handshake.

"Bob's going to make a killing off this," said Principal Barkin. "Do you know how many people will want to drink milk from a green cow with purple spots?"

Miles grimaced. "How many?"

"A lot!" said Principal Barkin. "Probably a lot of people, I bet!" He leaned back in his chair, which squeaked. "I wonder if the milk is green."

"Or purple," said Niles.

"Interesting point, Niles!" said Principal Barkin.

"Or just white still," said Miles.

Principal Barkin frowned.

"Show some imagination, Miles."

The principal looked at the article and shook his head.

"I mean, how does a cow become green overnight? With purple spots!"

"Maybe someone painted it," Miles said.

"Who would paint a cow?"

"How should I know?" said Miles.

"*How should I know?* Is that your new catchphrase, Miles?"

"No," said Miles.

"Ah!" said Principal Barkin. "So is it available as a catchphrase?"

"Principal Barkin," said Niles, "is this why you called us to your office? To talk about cows? Because we love talking about cows—"

"Who doesn't!" said Principal Barkin.

"—but we have class right now."

"Yeah," said Miles, "and we know how you feel about students missing instructional time."

"I hate students missing instructional time!" said Principal Barkin.

"Right," said Miles. "We know."

"However," said Principal Barkin, "this is important."

He leaned back in his chair again, and it squeaked again. Principal Barkin smiled.

"Notice anything different about me?"

Miles and Niles took a good look at their principal.

Principal Barry Barkin was a man who changed very little. He was devoted to routines. He woke up at the same time every day (precisely one minute before his alarm went off). He ate the same breakfast (oatmeal on toast). Every three weeks, he went to the barbershop, where he asked for the same haircut ("Clean it up around the sides, Paul.") and made the same joke ("Don't touch the top."). He wore the same suit. He wore the same shoes. When those shoes wore out, he bought the same pair. "A POWERFUL PRINCIPAL PLOTS A PATH AND NEVER STRAYS FROM IT." That was principle six in *The Seven Principles of Principal Power*, a book that Barkin brought with him wherever he went.

But now he was asking what was different about him.

Miles stared.

Niles squinted.

Principal Barkin was delighted by the attention.

Here is Principal Barkin on the first day of school two years ago, when Miles Murphy first arrived in Yawnee Valley:

And this is him exactly two years later, sitting across from Miles and Niles in the same office, in the same squeaky chair.

Take a good look. Notice anything different?

Niles's eyes widened and he smiled brightly.

"Your tie!"

"Correct, Niles!" said Principal Barkin.

If you guessed that Principal Barkin's tie was a different color, you're absolutely right!

If you didn't guess, well, you know, it's probably because we can't afford to print these books in color.

But anyway, here's the deal: Every year, on the first day of school, Principal Barkin wore the same tie. It was his favorite tie, and it was bright red, which, according to *The Seven Principles of Principal Power*, was the Official Color of Powerful Principals. This powerful tie had a small yellow mustard stain, but you couldn't see that unless you looked from very close up. At a distance, it was pure power red, glowing like the eye of an angry beast, or the hole of a rumbling volcano.

The first day of school was when Principal Barkin always gave his annual power speech, an address that "kicked the year off right" by "establishing his absolute authority over the school." Over the years, Principal Barkin's speeches had covered many topics. There was "Don't Just Hear. *Listen.* (To Me, Your Principal, Principal Barkin.)" The next year was "The Other Three Rs: Respect, Responsibility, and Really Good Attitude."

And of course there was the time Principal Barkin used his speech to introduce Yawnee Valley Science and Letters Academy's Positive Student Behavior Program, called M.U.N.C.H. (**M**ake good choices, **U**se quiet voices, **N**ever question your principal, **C**hoices!, **H**ands and feet to yourself.)

Principal Barkin's red tie was an important part of a successful power speech, since, like his words, it conveyed pure power. (Students couldn't see the mustard stain from where they sat in the auditorium. Principal Barkin knew this because one time, over the summer, when nobody was around, he'd put the tie on a CPR dummy propped up onstage behind a podium, then tested the views from various seats. No matter where he sat, that dummy looked powerful!)

So yes, on the first day of school, Principal Barkin always wore a red tie.

But today, this morning, the morning of the first day of school, Principal Barkin's tie was purple. Purple!

Principal Barkin smiled.

"Now Niles, you will probably also have noticed, and Miles, you are less likely to have noticed since you don't really seem to pay attention to these things, that it is 8:45 in the morning, and we three are sitting here in my office, when normally we, and all your classmates, would be—"

"In the auditorium, listening to a power speech," said Miles.

"Wow," said Principal Barkin. "Miles. You did notice."

Miles celebrated with a little pump of his fist.

"You see, boys," said Principal Barkin, "something has changed in me. Not just the color of my necktie, which is something that has changed *on* me, technically, but the nature of my soul, which, like a necktie, is altered. Over the last two years, something has been happening to me, has been happening *in* me, which my wife, Mrs. Barkin, says happens to a lot of men my age, but I think she is wrong. Because the things that have happened to me are *unusual*. My car was parked on the top of the stairs, which, Miles, in light of recent revelations, I am now starting to believe once again you did, and I still don't know how you did it."

"I didn't," said Miles.

"Also, remember when I was placed on an involuntary, indefinite leave of absence? I was out of a job, thanks largely to you two, but then I was back into a job, the same job, also thanks largely to you two. And then there was the time I fell into a large hole in the woods, which was the start of a summertime adventure! What I am trying to say is, we have been through a lot, we three. We are linked, me, and you, and you, and in many ways one could say that your club, the Terrible Twos—"

"The Terrible Two," said Niles.

"—the Terrible Two, has transformed—like a pupa, or one of those toys, what are they called, the ones they make all the movies of, a Transformer—transformed, like a Transformer, into a new, slightly larger club, one with the same initials, T.T.: The Terrible Three!"

"Hmmm," said Niles.

"And one could also say, and in fact I am saying it, that I also feel transformed! Whereas once I was a Powerful Principal, this year, I have decided to become a new kind of principal, again, one with the same initials, P.P.—"

"Hmmm," said Miles.

"A Pranking Principal!"

Principal Barkin was grinning wildly.

"And boys, *that* is why I have called you to my office. To talk, just us three pranksters, and to tell you that this morning I played a prank!"

Miles and Niles were more than a little stunned.

"How did it go?" Niles asked.

"It went great!" said Principal Barkin.

GREAT WAS OVERSELLING IT.

The prank had gone down at the morning faculty meeting. At 7:00 in the morning, the staff of Yawnee Valley Science and Letters Academy was required to gather in the teachers' lounge to go over important items for the year ahead: enrollment statistics, safety protocols, new rules for the teacher bathroom. Doughnuts were provided.

By 6:55 A.M., twenty-three bleary teachers were sitting around a big oak table. Ms. Shandy was enjoying a maple bar. A cruller sat on a napkin in front of Mrs. Trieber, untouched. The sides of Mr. Maxwell's mouth were dusted white; he was halfway through a powdered sugar. Ms. Machle licked her fingers in between bites of a sugar glazed. Ms. Lewis, as usual, had arrived early and grabbed the only morning bun. Mr. Gebott, wondering once again why Principal Barkin did not provide more morning buns, settled for several cinnamon doughnut holes, which he arranged in a little pyramid. Coach B. was on his second strawberry frosted.

Coach O. was removing a brown paper bag from the staff fridge.

"Going to have your morning hard-boiled egg, Tom?" Principal Barkin said, and then winked.

"Yeah," said Coach O. "Did you just wink at me?"

"No!" said Principal Barkin. "Why would I do that?"

He then turned to the table and winked at all the other teachers.

"Hmmm," said Ms. Shandy.

Barkin, who had wheeled his chair to the teachers' lounge from his office, buried his face in a pamphlet called *1,349 Interesting Things You May or May Not Know about Cows, Second Edition, Revised and Updated with a Few New Facts, and without Several Facts from the Previous Edition That Turned Out to Not Be True.*

"Well!" Principal Barkin exclaimed as he dunked an old-fashioned in a mug of coffee. "Huh! Huh, huh huh. Would you believe that!"

"OK," said Ms. Shandy. "What is it, Barry?"

"Well, since you asked," said Principal Barkin, "listen to this. 'Fact 316: There are 1.5 billion cows on planet Earth.'"

"So?" asked Coach O.

"SO?" said Principal Barkin.

Coach O., frowning, set his bag on the table and took out a hard-boiled egg. For the last year and a half, Coach O. had been on a low-carb diet. Not coincidentally, he'd also been in an eighteen-month-long bad mood, which got worse when he was surrounded by doughnuts.

"So what?" said Coach O. "Who would want to know how many cows there are on planet Earth?"

(Well, someone who had read the first chapter of this book might want to know that, for example.)

"WHO WOULD WANT TO KNOW HOW MANY COWS THERE ARE ON PLANET EARTH!" Principal Barkin's face turned a little bit purple, the color of a thistle. "I WOULD WANT TO KNOW HOW MANY COWS THERE ARE ON PLANET EARTH, TOM. IN FACT, I DID WANT TO KNOW, AND THEN I JUST FOUND OUT!"

"That makes one of us," said Coach O.

"OH, JUST EAT YOUR EGG, TOM," said Principal Barkin.

"How many people are there on planet Earth?" asked Mr. Stevenson (jelly doughnut).

"About 7.5 billion," said Ms. Shandy, who taught social studies.

"That's five people for every cow!" said Ms. Machle, who taught math.

"Wow," said Mr. Gebott, "I would have thought there were more cows on Earth than people."

There were murmurs of agreement from various teachers, and murmurs of disagreement from other teachers.

"I wonder if there are more people on Earth, or dogs," said Mrs. Thoren (chocolate frosted).

"Dogs," said Ms. Lewis. "Definitely."

Mr. Gebott shook his head. "I bet people!"

"Do stray dogs count?" asked Mr. Maxwell.

"Why wouldn't they?" asked Mrs. Trieber, who owned seven rescue dogs and was offended by the question.

"I think there are more dogs in Linda's house than people on Earth," said Ms. Shandy.

Everybody laughed, except Mrs. Trieber, whose first name was Linda.

"What about starfish?" asked Mr. Gebott. "Starfish or people?"

Coach O. sighed as he placed his egg on a ceramic eggcup. He had a system for eating a hard-boiled egg: He'd tap its top with a tiny spoon to carefully crack the shell; once all the pieces of eggshell had been removed and swept into a little plastic bag to be thrown away later, Coach O. would set the naked egg back atop the eggcup; he'd then use the side of the spoon to slice the egg in half and lightly sprinkle salt (from a shaker he kept in the lounge) onto both sides before popping them, one by one, into his mouth. If he had to eat a hard-boiled egg while everyone else downed doughnuts, he might as well enjoy the process. He removed his silver spoon from his sweatpants pocket.

Principal Barkin was watching him.

"How's that egg, Tom?" Barkin asked.

"I don't know, Barry," said Coach O. "I haven't even cracked it yet."

Principal Barkin grinned. "Well, don't let me keep you!"

"He just winked again," said Ms. Shandy.

"No I didn't!" said Principal Barkin, who had.

"Shouldn't we start?" said Ms. Machle.

It was 7:04.

"Ah!" said Principal Barkin. "Yes, let us get under way! Feel free to finish your doughnut, or egg, as the case may be, as we embark on this morning's meeting. First up, testing!"

The teachers groaned.

"Testing will commence as usual in . . . in . . ." said Principal Barkin, whose gaze flickered between the agenda in his hands and Coach O., who'd raised his spoon over his egg.

Coach O. noticed the principal trailing off and looked up.

"In October," said Principal Barkin. "You'll notice I've included a graph . . . of past results in your . . . your packets . . ."

Coach O.'s silver spoon once again hovered in the airspace just above his egg.

"Your packets . . ." said Principal Barkin, "your packets, which thanks again, Janet, for . . . for collating on such short notice—"

Coach O. gave the egg three sharp taps. The shell cracked, and egg white flew forth in all directions, splattering on the table.

Ms. Lewis yelped.

Mr. Gebott snorted.

Ms. Machle said, "Ha, ha!" (She actually said it.)

Bright orange yolk ran down the side of the eggcup and

pooled around its base. Coach O. wiped the spoon off on his sweatpants and used a word that is acceptable in the teachers' lounge but not elsewhere in school, nor in the pages of this book.

Principal Barkin covered his mouth with the agenda, but it was still easy to tell he was laughing.

"Barry," said Coach O., "did you replace my hard-boiled egg with a raw one?"

"What!" said Principal Barkin. "Why would you think I did that?"

"Because of all the winking," said Coach O.

"What do you mean winking?" said Principal Barkin. "I mean, who ever heard of a pranking principal?"

"Not bad, Barry," said Ms. Shandy, who was being generous.

"Are my eggs still in there?" asked Coach O., on his way back to the fridge.

"I mean really," said Principal Barkin, "a principal who played a practical yolk? I mean, a practical *joke*!"

He winked.

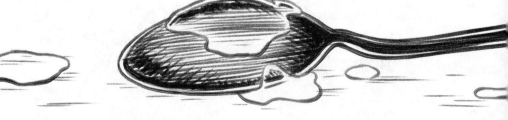

"WHY DID YOU KEEP WINKING at everyone?" asked Niles, back in the principal's office, once Barkin had finished his story.

"Because!" said Principal Barkin. "It was one of those, what does Niles call them, a, a—"

"A masterstroke?" said Miles.

"No," said Principal Barkin. "No, no. Niles, what do you call them?"

"A masterstroke," said Niles.

"Yes!" said Principal Barkin. "It was the masterstroke!"

"That's not what a masterstroke is," said Niles.

"Yeah," said Miles.

"Oh," said Principal Barkin. "I see. What's a masterstroke?"

"A masterstroke is a little extra prank on top of your prank. Like a grace note."

"Ah, yes!" Principal Barkin smiled. Then he frowned. "A grace note?"

"You know," said Miles, "notes you just add on yourself to the end of a tune, to make the whole thing prettier."

Miles whistled a pretty melody, punctuated by a few warbling notes that made the little ditty even prettier.

Principal Barkin clapped his hands together. "That was lovely! Rachmaninoff, right?"

"Chopin," said Miles.

Niles smiled. "I think Miles might be one of the world's greatest whistlers."

Miles shrugged. "I'm a prodigy."

Principal Barkin opened his bottom desk drawer and pulled out another notebook, this one embossed with the word FORMS. "Look at this. My pranking notebook."

Principal Barkin wrote down some notes about masterstrokes and grace notes and Chopin.

"So if my winking wasn't a masterstroke," he said, "then what was it?"

"I think it was just weird," said Niles.

"Ah," said Principal Barkin. "Right." He wrote down "weird" and snapped the notebook shut.

"Niles, Miles, I have learned a lot from you this morning. And I thank you. Many teachers will tell you that it is actually the *students* who teach *them*, which usually is just something they say to sound approachable, or profound, and which I find obnoxious. But this morning, as on many other occasions, you two, who are students, actually have taught me something. But then again, I am not a teacher, I am a principal. Anyway, what I am trying to say is, I wish you weren't graduating this year, and that things could stay this way forever."

Miles and Niles did not know what to say. So they both said, "Thanks."

"You are welcome," said Principal Barkin. "So. Do you want to stay here forever?"

"Here?" said Miles. "At Yawnee Valley Science and Letters Academy?"

"Yes," said Principal Barkin. "Or at least a few more years. Think of all the adventures we could still have! Like we could all go on a field trip, and there could be a big prank. A museum prank! Oh man. Or! Or what if somebody else started pulling pranks, and they were bad pranks, but everybody thought it was you guys doing them? And then the three of us had to team up, and we exposed the impostor! That would be exciting. Especially if the impostor was Josh Barkin, who is my son! Complicated. Or . . . I don't know . . . something with Christmas?"

"Uh," said Miles. "What?"

"Yeah, like I could put on a Christmas pageant, although actually it would probably have to be a holiday pageant, and then you two could prank it. You know? I don't know. Merry Prankmas! No. Sorry. Pranky holidays!"

"Ummm," said Niles.

Luckily, at that moment, the phone rang.

OR MAYBE UNLUCKILY.

Principal Barkin picked up his phone.

"HELLO, BARRY. THIS IS YOUR FATHER, FORMER PRINCIPAL BARKIN. I HOPE I AM NOT INTERRUPTING YOU—"

"Actually, Dad, I'm in a meeting right now but—"

"DO NOT INTERRUPT ME," said Former Principal Barkin. "BARRY, IS THERE A COPY OF TODAY'S NEWSPAPER ON YOUR DESK RIGHT NOW?"

"Of course there is, Dad."

Back before Principal Barkin was a principal, when he was just a kid called Little Barry Barkin, his father, Former

Principal Barkin (who at that time was a principal called Principal Barkin) required his sons to read the newspaper every day, top to bottom, front to back, minus the comic strips, which he called the funnies, and which he hated. Their father had a saying: "The only thing worse than a lazy soldier is a talking dog, and you'll find both in the funnies." And he had another saying: "The funnies promote the idea that laughter is the best medicine, when in fact preventive care is the best medicine. A careful diet, vigorous exercise, and regular checkups have saved far more lives than the funnies have." Also he had this saying: "'The funnies' is a ridiculous term and I do not like the way it feels in my mouth. So I am tired of telling you, Barry: Stop reading the funnies with a flashlight in your closet. Do not deny it. Your fingers give you away. They are constantly smeared with colorful ink, and the funnies are the only pages printed in color, which is a waste of money. Show me your fingers, Barry. SHOW ME! I knew it. Disgusting. Throw the funnies away, and then go wash your hands. I wish you were more like your brother, Bob."

Anyway, back to the phone call: "WELL THEN I'M SURE YOU KNOW WHY I AM CALLING YOU RIGHT NOW, BARRY."

Niles mouthed "Should we leave?" and pointed to the door.

Principal Barkin shook his head while he continued to talk on the phone. "Yes, yes, Bob's cow turned green. Hooray for Bob. Great for Bob. Another victory for Bob. Can't wait to see the smug look on his smug face next time I—"

"Hey, bro," said Bob Barkin.

"Bob?" said Principal Barkin. "Why are you on this call?"

"I'm driving with Dad right now. You're on speaker."

"You're together? Where are you driving?"

"DON'T TELL HIM, BOB," said Former Principal Barkin.

"Ah," said Principal Barkin. "Well, congratulations on the cow, Bob. Although it's probably just painted."

"OF COURSE THE COW IS JUST PAINTED, BARRY," said Former Principal Barkin. "BUT THE QUESTION IS THIS: WHO WOULD PAINT A COW?"

"How should I know?" said Principal Barkin.

"TELL HIM, BOB."

"Aliens," said Bob Barkin.

"Aliens?" said Principal Barkin.

"ALIENS," said Former Principal Barkin. "THERE ARE CROP CIRCLES ALL OVER BOB'S FARM."

"Crop circles?" said Principal Barkin.

"PATTERNS CUT INTO THE LANDSCAPE, BARRY. EVIDENCE OF EXTRATERRESTRIAL LIFE."

"Polka dots," said Bob. "Right there in the pasture. Same pattern as on the cow, actually. My best guess right now is that they're trying to send humanity some sort of message, through my farm, you know?"

Again, below the desk, Miles and Niles exchanged a secret handshake.

(In case you were wondering what that lawn mower was for back on page 5, it was for the masterstroke.)

"Unbelievable," said Principal Barkin.

"The paper's running another front-page story tomorrow," said Bob.

"PRETTY NEAT, EH?" said Former Principal Barkin.

"Why would aliens visit Bob's farm?" said Principal Barkin.

"WELL IF EXTRATERRESTRIALS WERE

GOING TO TRAVEL LIGHT-YEARS ACROSS THE UNIVERSE TO VISIT ONE OF THE BARKIN BROTHERS, WHO DO YOU THINK THEY WOULD PICK? YOUR BROTHER, BOB, WHO RUNS A

SUCCESSFUL DAIRY, OR YOU, BARRY, A FAILED PRINCIPAL WHO STRUGGLES TO MAINTAIN EVEN A LOOSE GRIP ON HIS SCHOOL?"

"Bob, I guess," said Principal Barkin.

"THAT'S RIGHT. BOB."

"Is this why you called me, Dad?" asked Principal Barkin. "To talk about cows? Because I love talking about cows—"

"Who doesn't!" said Bob Barkin.

"—but I'm in the middle of something important."

"SOMETHING IMPORTANT?" said Former Principal Barkin. "*SOMETHING IMPORTANT?* WHAT COULD BE MORE IMPORTANT THAN A CONVERSATION WITH YOUR FATHER? YOUR BROTHER, BOB, CLEARED HIS SCHEDULE TODAY, A DAY WHEN HE IS IN THE CENTER OF A MAJOR NEWS STORY AND POSSIBLE INTERPLANETARY CONTACT EVENT, JUST TO TAKE A DRIVE WITH ME."

"Uh-huh," said Principal Barkin.

"BUT NO, BARRY, I DID NOT CALL TO TALK TO YOU ABOUT COWS, OR BOB, OR EXTRATERRESTRIALS. IS THE NEWSPAPER STILL ON YOUR DESK?"

"Yes, Dad."

"TAKE A GANDER AT PAGE A16."

Principal Barkin paged through to the back of the newspaper. Page A16 was where they ran the obituaries—notices of the recent deaths of national figures and Yawnee Valley locals—and the BrainBunglers, a collection of crossword puzzles, word searches, and scramblers.

Principal Barkin rolled his eyes. "Come on, Dad! You know I don't do the BrainBunglers."

"I'M NOT TALKING ABOUT THE BRAINBUN-GLERS. LOOK AT THE OBITS, BARRY."

Principal Barkin scanned the obituaries. A nuclear scientist. The ex-president of a large South American country. The inventor of a popular stapler.

"Oh," said Principal Barkin. "Oh my."

He laid the newspaper back down on his desk.

"THAT'S RIGHT."

Niles craned his neck and tried to read the paper.

"What is it?"

"Harriet Nervig died," Principal Barkin said softly.

Niles sat up straight. "Harriet Nervig died?"

"YES," said Former Principal Barkin, "HARRIET NERVIG DIED."

"WAIT, WHO'S Harriet Nervig?" Miles asked.

It was a very good question! Because unless you possessed an intimate knowledge of the Yawnee Valley Unified School District, which Miles Murphy did not (and you probably don't either), you would have no idea who Harriet Nervig was. And if you had no idea who Harriet Nervig was, you might wonder why news of her death made your principal go pale. You might puzzle over the fact that your best friend's jaw had dropped. You might even think that last chapter ended with a pretty weak cliff-hanger.

So: Who was Harriet Nervig? According to her obituary,

Harriet Nervig—who, don't worry, died of natural causes, in her sleep, at the satisfying conclusion of a pleasant dream—was an avid camper and mezzo-soprano with certificates in both armed and unarmed stage combat. More to the point, for the last seventeen years, Harriet Nervig had been the superintendent of Yawnee Valley schools. She was, as her friends called her, the "big cheese." (Harriet was also an amateur cheesemaker.) And since Harriet Nervig had died—peacefully, of old age!—two years before the end of her fourth term, that meant, according to bylaw 139(f), as well as standing rule 22(c), which together established a rather

complicated line of succession for superintendents in the YVUSD—

"THAT MEANS I AM NOW SUPERINTENDENT, AND NOT JUST YOUR FATHER BUT YOUR BOSS."

"Oh my," said Principal Barkin.

"GIVE JOSH AND SHARON MY LOVE."

The man formerly known as Former Principal Barkin, now known as Acting Superintendent Barkin, hung up the phone, loudly. He was a busy man. Now that he was superintendent, there were bus schedules to approve. There were pie charts to print out on huge posters. And of course, there was his long-promised revenge on the Terrible Two to enact.

Now that's a cliff-hanger.

Chapter 12

PRINCIPAL BARKIN ROCKED in his chair, which squeaked sadly.

"Well," said Principal Barkin, "this is not good. In fact, it is really bad."

The door to his office flew open.

Acting Superintendent Barkin loomed in the doorway. A thin smiled formed on the old man's lips.

"Dad?" said Principal Barkin. "You were driving *here?*"

"I wanted to see the look on your face," said Acting Superintendent Barkin. "Plus I came for the portraits."

"The portraits?" said Principal Barkin.

"The portraits. Now that I am superintendent, I will of course be hanging the Barkins in my office. Our forefathers should be frowning down on me, not you. Bob, take them down."

"Hey, bro." Bob Barkin stepped into the principal's office and went to the back wall. Acting Superintendent Barkin nodded grimly as Bob removed the paintings of former principals, one by one.

Thadius Barkin

Roger Barkin

and, of course, Bertrand
Barkin himself.

"You can leave Barry up there," said Superintendent Barkin. "I don't want him."

"Got it, Dad."

Bob Barkin took a long look at the portrait of his brother.

"Say, Barry, did you do this one?"

Principal Barkin was staring at his desk.

"Yeah."

Bob whistled. "It's good!"

Principal Barkin did not look up.

"Thanks."

Acting Superintendent Barkin rolled his eyes.

"Yes, Barry, perhaps you should have been a painter. While that would have been extremely embarrassing to have a son who is an artist, it would have been far less embarrassing than having a son who is a weak principal. Your brother, Bob, could have carried on the family tradition. I have long suspected that he is the one made of real principal material."

"Eh, I like the dairy, Dad." Bob Barkin, with an armful of paintings, stepped awkwardly past his brother, around Miles and Niles, and paused by the door. "See you Sunday, Barry."

(On the last Sunday of every month, the Barkins got together for dinner. It was an occasion nobody looked forward to.)

"Looking forward to it, Bob," said Principal Barkin.

Acting Superintendent Barkin took a last look around his son's office. When he regarded Miles and Niles, a horrible noise came from deep inside the old man's throat. It was something like a scoff but even haughtier, more disdainful. "Today, at the pinnacle of my career, I walk in on my own son, a Barkin, a *principal*, having a sit-down with two little twerps. Another disappointment. I'll let you get back to your 'important meeting,' Barry."

Acting Superintendent Barkin turned to leave.

"We were in trouble!" Miles offered. "He was yelling at us about some pranks we did!"

The old man spun around and leaned in close to Miles's face.

Miles could smell the coffee on his breath. He flinched.

"Which one are you?" asked Acting Superintendent Barkin.

"What?" said Miles.

"Miles or Niles?"

"Oh. I'm Miles."

The superintendent shook his head.

"The names are very similar. It makes it hard for everybody to keep track."

"Not for us," Miles said.

"*Do not talk back, boy.*" Old Man Barkin's face twisted into an angry grimace and his words came out like a hiss. Then he smiled, stood up straight, and ran his thumbs along his suspenders. "*Miles,* I was a principal for twenty-eight years. And then, as you will remember, I was a principal again, briefly, for about six months. Over that time, I developed a nose for dishonesty. I can smell mischief. I can sniff out shenanigans. And let me tell you: This whole office stinks."

And with that, Acting Superintendent Barkin made his exit.

For a few seconds, there was an awful stillness in the principal's office.

Miles and Niles did not know what to say.

The walls looked barren.

Barry Barkin seemed deflated.

He sighed.

"Well, Miles, it was very kind of you to lie for me, even though your plan did not work."

"Yeah," said Miles. "Sorry."

Niles attempted a cheerful grin. He gestured to the wall.

"I didn't know you did that!"

"Yes," said Principal Barkin. "It's a self-portrait."

"It's good! You really captured you!"

"Thank you, Niles. My grandpa Jimmy loved to paint. He used to give me lessons when I was a boy, until my father found out and put an end to them. My dad had a saying: 'The arts are a wonderful way to fill your free time, and any person who has free time is indolent and therefore unworthy of respect.' But my grandfather was a real artist. He used to say that I had the gift, that it skipped a generation, but I think he was just being nice. He was a nice man."

"Well I think it's really good too," said Miles.

"Thank you, Miles," said Principal Barkin. "That compliment means a lot, almost as much as the compliment from Niles, who has an A in art."

"I have an A–!" Miles said.

"Yes," said Principal Barkin.

Niles stepped in. "Well, look on the bright side: At least you still have your portrait of you!"

Principal Barkin nodded. "That is true, Niles, that is true. On the one hand, I get to hold on to my painting, which I am very proud of. On the other hand, my father did not want that painting, which I am proud of, in his new office. I am not sure whether I should feel grateful, or devastated, so I think I will feel both things at the same time."

The bell rang.

"You boys better get back to class."

Niles and Miles stood up.

Niles had the face he always had when he was thinking hard. This face:

When Niles was thinking hard, he sometimes forgot where he was. He left the room without saying good-bye. And so Miles, who tended to cover for his friend when he was distracted, said good-bye for both of them.

"Later, Principal B.!"

Then he ran down the hall to find out what Niles was thinking about.

"S0?" MILES ASKED in the hallway. "What are you thinking about?"

"Not now," said Niles. "After school."

And so 3:30 P.M. found Miles and Niles in the prank lab, a walk-in closet attached to Niles's bedroom. From the outside, the prank lab looked like a normal closet. But inside, it was chaos, and mayhem, and mischief. The walls of the prank lab were covered in chalkboard paint so they could write down their schemes. Ideas for pranks. Names of people who needed a good pranking. Lists of necessary pranking equipment. The one thing that never got erased from the walls was the Prankster's Oath, which Niles said was the official pledge of a secret pranking society called the International Order of Disorder, but which Miles was pretty sure Niles had just made up:

On my honor I will do my best
To be good at being bad;

To disrupt, but not destroy;

To embarrass the dour and amuse the merry;

To devote my mind to japes, capers, shenanigans, and monkey business;

To prove the world looks better turned upside down;

For I am a prankster.

So be it.

(If you want, you can swear yourself in. Just raise your left hand and say these words aloud.)

Miles loved the prank lab. It was like being inside Niles's brain. Although after two years, a lot of the stuff on the walls was stuff Miles had written. So it was like being inside both their brains at the same time, or a joint brain that could only be made by melding their minds together. But speaking of being inside Niles's brain, Miles asked, again, "What are you thinking about?"

"A prank."

"Yeah, obviously," said Miles. "But what's the prank?"

"I don't know yet," said Niles. "I feel like I have the pieces, but I'm still arranging them."

"Who's the goat?" Miles asked.

"You know who the goat is."

"Yeah," said Miles. "I know who the goat is."

(A goat, in the S.P.L. of the Terrible Two, does not refer to an animal with horns. It is not short for the Greatest of All Time. A goat is somebody who gets pranked.)

"The goat is Old Man Barkin, right?" said Miles.

"Yes," said Niles. He was staring at the ceiling.

"Back to war with our old foe!" said Miles.

"No," said Niles. "A superintendent can't do anything to us. I think that job is just filling out forms."

"Oh," said Miles. "Then why—"

"Did you see the way he talked to Principal Barkin? I don't like it."

"Yeah," said Miles. "But—"

"I don't like it one bit."

"It's not really our business though."

Niles sat up. "Of course it's our business! It's at least a little bit our business. Principal Barkin is a prankster now."

Miles frowned.

"At least he could be a prankster now," said Niles. "Or one day. In the future. What I'm saying is there's potential."

"Maybe," said Miles.

"Miles," said Niles. "This is our last year at Yawnee Valley

Science and Letters Academy. And, yeah, it's our job to enjoy it. And, next year, after we graduate, we get to go to a new school together—"

"Unless I go to St. Perpetua," said Miles.

"What? Why would your mom send you to St. Perpetua?" Niles asked. "You guys aren't even Catholic."

"I know," Miles said. "I was just joking."

"I don't get it."

"I don't know," said Miles.

"Miles," said Niles. "I'm in the middle of a speech. Now. Next year, when we graduate, we get to go to a new school together. But what is our legacy?"

"Our legacy?"

"What do we leave behind? What is the thing that lasts forever?"

"Oh," said Miles. "Wow."

They sat in the prank lab and thought in silence.

"What do you think it will be like?" Miles said. "Next year?"

"I don't know," Niles said. "I think it will be different. And the same."

"It's like we're going over a waterfall," said Miles. "In a barrel. But at least we're going over the waterfall together. There's nobody I'd rather be in a barrel with than you. Although I guess

we're all going over the waterfall, everybody in our class. In different barrels, probably. You couldn't fit us all in one barrel. But we would fit in one barrel, you and me, even if it's a tight squeeze."

"You sound like Principal Barkin," Niles said.

Miles gasped. "I *do* sound like Principal Barkin."

And they laughed about that for a while.

Then Niles said, "Enough about next year! Let's think about this year." He erased a section of the wall with his sleeve and started to write.

THREE WEEKS went by. Miles and Niles went through one tub of red licorice in the prank lab. They tried a tub of black licorice next. Niles liked it. Miles didn't. At school, hot lunches got served cold. Students started wearing puffy coats. The secretaries changed the decorations on the front office's bulletin board from apples to pumpkins. Time moved forward. Time marched on. Time flew by. But who had time to think about time, with all the constant homework and emergency drills and changing for P.E.?

Miles and Niles changed for P.E.

"Hey, GUYS! Hey, MILES! Hey, NILES! Hey, PRANKERS!"

"Hey, Stuart," said Miles and Niles, at the same time.

Niles swung his locker door shut and resigned himself to putting on his gym clothes. He removed his tie, then his shirt, then carefully folded each and arranged them neatly on a bench.

"Check. It. OUT!" said Stuart. "My MOM bought me DEODORANT!"

Stuart held a stick of deodorant aloft, like a torch.

"Cool, man," said Miles.

"Yeah," said Niles.

"I'm not really SWEATING yet, but when we were in the STORE I asked my MOM and she said YES!"

There were four kinds of kids in the locker rooms of Yawnee Valley Science and Letters Academy. Some kids needed to wear deodorant and wore it. (Miles Murphy was one of these kids.) Some kids needed to wear deodorant but didn't wear it. (Josh Barkin had been one of these kids for at least two years.) Some kids did not need to wear deodorant and didn't wear it. (Niles Sparks.) And some kids did not need to wear deodorant but really wanted to and convinced their parents to buy it for them anyway.

"I just like the way it SMELLS!" said Stuart. "I guess for ME, it's ODORANT!"

Stuart laughed hard at his own joke, which was nice, because nobody else did.

"It's WATERFALL SCENTED!" Stuart said. "LOOK!"

Indeed, the deodorant's label featured a roaring cataract and spumy clouds.

"I was TRYING FOREVER to decide between WATER-FALL and AVALANCHE, and then I was like, WAIT, what does an AVALANCHE even SMELL like? You KNOW?"

"Yeah, but what does a waterfall smell like?" Niles asked.

Stuart frowned. He uncapped his deodorant and sniffed it. "THIS, I guess!"

Stuart passed the stick to Niles, who held it below his nose.

"Huh," said Niles. It smelled like baby powder.

"Well, well, well," said Josh Barkin, sidling up to Niles's locker. (It was getting pretty crowded around there.) Josh set his school clothes down in a heap on top of Niles's neat stack. "What is this, is there a nimbus convention in town or something?"

"Hey, Josh," said Miles and Niles and Stuart, at the same time, except Stuart said it like this: "Hey, JOSH!"

"Well lookie here." Josh was eyeing Niles. "The littlest nimbus is *finally* wearing deodorant, like a big nimbus." He pretended to wipe a tear from his eye. "They grow up so fast. Here, nimbus, let me show you how to use it."

He snatched the deodorant out of Niles's hand.

"It's not mine, Josh," said Niles.

"You don't even WEAR deodorant, Josh," said Stuart.

"I don't need to, nimbus. My sweat smells *good*. Now, Niles Nimbus, pay close attention. At the bottom of your deodorant, you'll find a little wheel, which you turn like so. That's what makes the deodorant pop up."

With his thumb and forefinger, Josh clumsily spun the plastic wheel on the deodorant's case. A fragrant white bar poked up.

"It's a miracle!" said Josh. "The more you spin, the more deodorant you get! A stinky little nimbus like you is probably going to need *a lot* of deodorant."

Faster and faster, Josh twisted the little plastic wheel. The deodorant cake continued to slowly emerge. Josh furrowed his brow and wrinkled his nose. This was taking longer than he'd planned on, and he'd run out of intimidating patter. "Um, uh, like *a lot a lot*, so I'll just keep twisting . . ."

"Give it back, Josh," said Niles.

"Yeah, GIVE IT!" said Stuart. He grabbed for his deodorant, but Josh fended him off by pushing his palm into Stuart's face.

"It's not *mine*, Josh," said Niles.

But Josh did not hear Niles. He ignored Stuart's pleas. For Josh Barkin was now in a frenzy. The cruel joy of his endeavor had driven him berserk. He kept clicking the little plastic wheel.

At last, the cake of deodorant grew so long that it fell out of its case and plopped onto the ground.

"Oops!" said Josh.

Then he stepped on the deodorant cake and slid his foot slowly along the floor, leaving a thick white smear on the concrete. The whole area around Niles's locker smelled like a waterfall. (Or baby powder.)

"Double oops!" said Josh. "Sorry, Niles Nimbus."

"It wasn't mine, Josh."

"It was MINE!" said Stuart.

Josh looked at Stuart as if noticing him for the first time. "Oh. Sorry, nimbus. Collateral damage."

Stuart stared at the locker-room floor.

Josh pointed at Niles. "It's his fault. I thought the deodorant was his."

Josh sighed. "Well, now I gotta bust something of Niles's to make it even."

Josh Barkin bent over the bench, rummaging through the pile of clothes to try to find Niles's tie, which he planned to hold over his head and rip into two pieces. Maybe even three.

Then Josh stopped rummaging.

He paused.

"What the glug?" said Josh.

You may have wondered where Miles had gone during this whole episode of Josh and the deodorant stick. While Josh was spinning that plastic wheel, and Stuart was grasping, and Niles was protesting, what was Miles Murphy doing?

Josh held up a pair of jeans.

His own jeans, to be exact.

They were a normal pair of jeans, except for one thing. There was a combination lock looped through the buttonhole on the fly.

"WHO DID THIS?" Josh's face was turning purple, the color of certain carrots. "WHO DID IT?"

The boys in the locker room took a break from changing into their gym clothes, from throwing their socks at each other, from hiking Patrick Bergner's sneaker like a football. Everybody stopped to look at Josh's jeans. Then most of them started laughing.

"WHICH ONE OF YOU NIMBUSES LOCKED UP MY PANTS?" said Josh.

I mean, Miles Murphy had, obviously.

"IT WAS YOU, wasn't it, nimbus?"

Josh Barkin had his finger between two of Miles's ribs.

"I didn't do it," said Miles.

"Yes, you did," said Josh. "This is your lock."

Miles inspected the combination lock attached to Josh's jeans.

"Nope," he said. "I don't think so, Josh. I mean, locks do look alike, so I can't be 100 percent sure. But I know my lock pretty well, and this doesn't look like my lock."

"Then whose lock is it?"

"Why don't you ask everyone again?" Niles said.

"WHOSE LOCK IS ON MY PANTS, EVERYONE?" Josh asked.

Everybody laughed again, especially Miles and Niles. Stuart was really loving it.

"Actually, you know what, Josh?" said Miles. "I just realized. That *is* my lock."

Josh was panicking and getting sweaty.

"Unlock it, nimbus," he said.

"OK," Miles said.

He gave the dial a few spins.

Then he shook his head.

"I can't remember the combination."

"DO YOU WANT A BEATDOWN, NIMBUS?"

"Whoa, whoa," said Miles. "You're stressing me out. It's really hard to remember things when I'm stressed out."

Miles lowered his head and stood for a few seconds in silent contemplation.

His head snapped up.

"I can't remember," he said.

"NIMBUS!"

"Look on the bright side!" said Niles. "We've got P.E. right now, so you don't have to put those pants back on for another forty-five minutes!"

Josh was slapping his jeans against the bench, as if he could shake the lock off.

"You should just try some combinations and see if you can guess it," said Miles. "How many possibilities could there be?"

"60,840," said Niles.

"Oh," said Miles. "That's a lot. How long would that take?"

Niles considered the question.

"About six days. If you didn't sleep."

"He'll probably want to sleep," said Miles.

"Yeah," said Niles.

Josh grew purpler and sweat harder. Math made Josh sweat. He glistened, like an amethyst.

"I think there was a four in it."

"Well now we're down to 4,641!" said Niles.

"Or maybe it's a nine."

"9,282."

"Actually, forget it," Miles said. "I'm thinking of a different lock."

"Back to 60,840." Niles gave Josh a sympathetic look.

"I WILL POUND ALL YOU NIMBUSES!" Josh roared. "I WILL POUND YOU, AND I WILL ALSO TELL ON YOU. I AM TELLING COACH O. I AM TELLING COACH B. I AM TELLING MY DAD, WHO IS THE PRINCIPAL, AND MY GRANDFATHER, WHO IS NOW THE SUPERINTENDENT. YOU ARE GOING TO GET IN SO MUCH TROUBLE, AND ALSO YOU ARE GOING TO GET SO POUNDED."

"Why would I get in trouble?" Miles asked. "It was an accident."

"AN ACCIDENT?"

"Yeah," said Miles. "I had my lock on the bench. It probably just closed on your jeans when you put them down on the bench."

Niles nodded wisely. "From the rummaging, you're saying."

Miles agreed. "Exactly. From the rummaging."

"YOU EXPECT ME TO BELIEVE THAT? WHAT ARE THE CHANCES OF THAT HAPPENING?"

"One in 10,723," said Niles, which was a figure he'd just made up. He shrugged. "But more unlikely things have happened."

Nearby, in the gym, Coach O. and Coach B. blew their whistles wildly, signaling the start of P.E.

"Let's hustle, gentlemen!" said Coach B.

"Hustle, hustle!" said Coach O. "Show some hustle."

The boys in the locker room headed for the exit, jostling against each other, showing varying degrees of hustle.

Josh ran off to stuff his jeans in his locker.

Miles shared Niles's locker, since Miles no longer had a lock.

"Thanks, GUYS!" Stuart whispered, loudly. "That was COOL!"

Then Miles and Niles and Stuart joined the large clump of kids trying to squeeze through a small doorway.

Josh's head popped up amid the crowd. He found Miles and Niles and gave them a malicious grin.

"I hope today is something with sticks," he said.

"THE NAME OF THE GAME is lacrosse," said Coach O., after blowing his whistle. "We got a bigger equipment budget this year, which allowed us to buy some lacrosse sticks."

"Exciting," said Coach B.

"However," said Coach O., "the equipment budget was not big enough to cover lacrosse pads."

"Next year," said Coach B.

"Of course," said Coach O., "none of you will be here next year, unless you flunk or something."

"We call it 'repeating a grade' now, Tom," said Coach B., who'd been reprimanded on two occasions for using the word "flunking."

"Regardless," said Coach O., "for the time being, given our pad situation, we're going to need you all to exercise personal responsibility with these sticks."

"Yuss!" Josh pumped his arm.

"What's that, Barkin?" said Coach B.

"Just cheering for personal responsibility, Coach," Josh said.

"Gotcha."

Coach B. blew his whistle, then Coach O. did.

"Go grab your sticks!"

Josh ran over and tore open a mesh bag, elbowing out the other students as he searched for the biggest stick. (They were all the same size.)

Miles and Niles approached the coaches. They each handed Coach O. an envelope.

"What're these?" Coach O. asked.

"Letters from our doctors. I have hay fever," said Niles, who did.

"And I also have hay fever," said Miles, who didn't. (His letter was fake.)

"According to our doctors, we can't participate in sports on days when the pollen count is over 9." (Although Niles did have hay fever, his letter was also fake.)

"And what's the pollen count today?" Coach O. asked.

"It's 9.8," said Niles.

"Uh-huh," said Coach O. "Well, well. What're the odds, two friends, both with the same allergy?"

"It's difficult to say with certainty, Coach," said Niles, "but I'd guess they're better than you'd think! After all, friends tend

to have things in common. And when you look at it that way, our hay fever is sort of a shared affinity! Plus allergies in kids are on the rise generally, which experts think might be due to a lack of exposure to farm animals, which would certainly be true for Miles, or a lack of vitamin D, and I'd definitely describe myself as an indoor kid!"

"OK." Coach O. studied the letters. On the one hand, he thought they were probably fake. On the other hand, he'd seen a lot of fakes in his day, and these letters looked real—convincing letterhead, flowing signatures, and so on. On the third hand, Coach O. didn't really care. His gaze softened as he imagined what it would be like to have three hands. With three hands, he would have almost certainly made quarterback in college, and probably would have gone on to play pro ball. He'd be on the front of a cereal box right now, instead of trying to figure out if a couple of doctor's notes were forgeries.

"All right," said Coach O. "You two can dust the trophies. Assuming that doesn't set off your hay fever."

By the time Josh returned to center court, gripping a stick he thought was bigger than the others (but wasn't), Miles and Niles were gone.

Chapter 17

THE SPORTING GLORY of Yawnee Valley Science and Letters Academy took up four shelves in a glass-fronted cabinet. There were trophies topped with loving cups, shiny golfers, and cows. Several old pictures of athletes—some posing alone, some standing in teams—were taped up in the back. Sprinters, pitchers, forwards, and receivers.

Niles got the keys to the trophy case from Gus, the janitor. Gus gave them some dust rags too, but nobody—not Gus, not Miles, not Niles—expected the boys to do much dusting.

Miles and Niles stood before the open cabinet, examining the various trophies.

"Look at that one!" Niles pointed. "It's Old Man Barkin."

"Second place?" said Miles. "That's not fair. All the other trophies in here are for first place."

Niles shook his head. "Some people get to do whatever they want."

That made Niles mad, and it always would.

"You know what's weird?" said Miles. "I pass these trophies every day and I've never looked at them."

"Nobody does," said Niles. "Nobody cares."

Miles pointed to a picture of the 1933 Yawnee Valley Science and Letters Academy boys' volleyball team. "They care."

Miles and Niles studied the players. Their shorts were very high and their hairstyles were mostly odd, but their faces looked just like kids' faces today.

They were both thinking the same thing, but Miles was the one to say it.

"Man. These kids would be really old now. Most of them are probably dead."

"Crazy."

Niles leaned in close. "Look! That guy looks kind of like Stuart!"

Miles leaned in too. "Yeah! What if it was Stuart?"

"What if Stuart was a thousand years old?"

"And he never aged."

They both laughed at that.

"What if Stuart was sent back in time, to 1933, to save humanity?" said Miles.

"Or destroy it."

"Like the Terminator."

"Yeah, maybe Stuart's a cyborg."

"What do you like better, *Terminator One* or *Two?*"

"Mmmm," said Niles. "*One.*"

"Me too," said Miles.

(Neither of them had seen any of the Terminator movies. They weren't allowed.)

"Hasta la vista, baby," said Miles.

"I'll be back," said Niles.

Just then, Stuart came out to the hallway to get a drink of water.

He wiped off his mouth and nodded at Miles and Niles.

"Hey, GUYS!" he said.

"Hey, Stuart," said Miles and Niles, at the same time.

Stuart jogged off.

Miles and Niles looked at each other with wide eyes.

"That *can't* be a coincidence," said Miles.

"It's like he heard us."

"Supersonic hearing."

They turned back to the photograph.

"Maybe that really *is* Stuart," said Miles.

"Man," said Niles.

Stuart was not a time-traveling cyborg. He was just thirsty. But Miles and Niles both knew that.

"Hey," said Miles, "do you ever think about if you want to be buried or whatever, after you die?"

"Yeah," said Niles. "Do you?"

"Yeah. I want my grave to have a bunch of statues, you know?"

"Of what?"

"Um, maybe me? A real MILES MURPHY WAS HERE kind of thing."

"Like a mausoleum?"

"What's that?"

"One of those grave buildings."

"Yeah!"

Niles nodded. "I have this idea. In my will, I'm going to have all that stuff where I leave my money to my kids, my books to the library—"

"Can I have your stereo speakers?" Miles asked.

"Sure. And then at the end I'm going to mention this box. I'm going to say, 'In my closet, on the top shelf, behind all my hats, there is a shoebox full of my secrets, to be burned after my death. In the event of my unfortunate demise, my descendants are to take this to my backyard and burn it. Do not look inside. This is my last will and testament, et cetera et cetera, Niles Sparks.' And then when my kids and my grandkids all go to the yard, and they build a fire, and they put the box on it, it'll be full of fireworks."

Miles grinned. "Nice!"

"Yeah, it's going to be beautiful."

"It's like a prank from beyond the grave! It's like a master-stroke to *life*!"

"Yeah. You can't tell anyone, like my kids or my grandkids or anything. I wasn't even going to tell you."

They touched their fingertips together. "I'm glad you did."

Holly came out to the water fountain.

"Hey, guys," she said. "How's the dusting?"

"Fine," said Miles. "Hey, Holly, do you want to be buried after you die?"

"Yeah," said Holly. "I guess. I'm probably going to be pretty famous, so it would be nice for people to be able to visit me. How about you guys?"

"Mausoleum," said Miles.

"I want to be buried at the foot of a giant sequoia," said Niles, "like they have in California. Then I'd become the tree."

Holly joined them at the trophy case.

"Huh," said Holly. "I always pictured you two side by side, like Jack Lemmon and Walter Matthau."

"Who're they?" Miles asked.

"Movie stars. And best friends. Niles, you should write them down."

He did, in a notebook he always carried, even in his gym shorts, on a page titled HOLLY MOVIES TO WATCH.

"They were in a bunch of movies together. And they got

buried right next to each other. It's really sweet. Hey, that kid looks like Stuart!"

"What are you kids talking about?"

Gus was standing behind them.

"Death," said Miles and Niles and Holly, cheerfully, and at the same time.

Another adult might have been concerned, or upset, or even disturbed to come across three kids matter-of-factly discussing mausoleums and wills, graveyards and epitaphs. But Gus had been a school janitor for thirty-four years. He had spent decades listening in on students' conversations. He knew what kids talked about. He was very good at his job.

"I see," said Gus. He held out his hand. "Keys, please."

Niles tossed Gus the heavy key ring.

Gus inspected the trophy case.

"Still pretty dusty," he said.

"We didn't do any dusting," Niles confessed.

Gus chuckled. "To be fair, I haven't dusted this thing in years either. I never notice it."

"Nobody does," said Miles.

Gus locked the case.

They all four stood before the glass.

Gus cleared his throat. "'Vain the ambition of kings who seek by trophies and dead things to leave a living name behind and weave but nets to catch the wind.'"

"Totally," said Miles.

"'Behind' and 'wind' don't really rhyme," said Holly.

Gus smiled. "You're right. How about this? 'And while the great and wise decay, and all their trophies pass away, some sudden thought, some careless rhyme, still floats above the wrecks of time.'"

"How do you do that? Just quote stuff like that?" Niles asked.

"I read. I listen. I remember."

Gus left the kids standing there, thinking.

Again, he was very good at his job.

"**A**ND THE LARGEST of the pyramids," said Ms. Shandy, "was built by?"

"Khufu," said twenty-four of the twenty-five kids in Ms. Shandy's social studies class, at the same time.

"That's right." Ms. Shandy had drawn some pyramids on the chalkboard. All her students agreed: She was great at drawing. "Work on the Great Pyramid began in the fourth dynasty, around 2580 B.C.E., and it took more than—Josh, what are you doing?"

Josh was bent over in his seat, with his head under his desk, almost like he was lying in his own lap.

"I'm cracking a lock, Ms. Shandy," said Josh Barkin.

"Well, lift your head up and bring your eyes forward," said Ms. Shandy.

Josh sighed. "Ms. Shandy, you obviously don't know anything about lock cracking. I need to hear the clicking. How am I supposed to crack the lock if I can't hear the clicking?"

"What lock are we even talking about?" said Ms. Shandy.

"The lock on my pants," said Josh, which made 24/25ths of the students giggle. It even seemed like Ms. Shandy was about to smile.

Holly leaned over to Niles. "This was you guys, wasn't it?" she whispered.

Niles blushed. "This one was mostly Miles."

Miles shook his head. "It was us. Everything we do is together."

"Miles, this one was all you!"

"He's just being modest," said Miles. "Besides, I learned most of what I know from the master."

Holly nodded. "Nice."

Niles gave Miles a look like, *Why did you give me credit?*

Miles winked at Niles. A wink is a very complicated look, but this one meant something like, *You know exactly why I gave you credit, and you're welcome, buddy.*

"Well, Josh," said Ms. Shandy, "you can crack that lock on your own time. Right now, this is my time, and we're learning about Egypt."

"I already know all about Egypt," said Josh.

"Who built the Great Pyramid?"

"Uhhh," said Josh, still under the desk.

"Class?"

"Khufu," said 96 percent of the class.

"Is that why everybody keeps saying Khufu?" said Josh. "It's really messing with my concentration. I'd probably have this lock cracked already if you guys weren't saying Khufu all the time."

"Josh, eyes up. Now."

"Hold on, Ms. Shandy! I just heard a click!"

"Josh."

"I'll be with you in one second, Ms. Shandy."

Josh pressed his ear against the lock and fumbled with the dial, spinning right, then left, then right again. He yanked down hard on the casing.

"Dang."

Chapter 19

ACTING SUPERINTENDENT Bertrand Barkin smiled, looking at a picture of himself scowling.

"Higher," he said. "A little lower. And to the right."

Josh Barkin huffed and moved the painting along the wall. After school, Josh had gone to see his grandfather so he could tell on Miles and Niles. Instead he'd ended up redecorating his grandfather's new office in the just-christened Harriet Nervig Memorial Yawnee Valley District Office Building.

"Left. Left. Perfect. Thank you, Josh. You may place it there."

Josh marked the spot on the wall with a pencil and looked around for a hammer.

"Now," said Acting Superintendent Barkin. "What's that hanging from your pants?"

"A lock."

"I see. Is this a . . . *fashion statement?*"

"No. It's a prank."

Acting Superintendent Barkin scowled (just like in his picture). "I see."

"Miles did it."

"Is Miles the little blond?"

"No, it's the other one. The new kid, who's not new any-more."

Acting Superintendent Barkin sighed. "I wish their names were more different. It makes it so hard to tell them apart."

"Not for me," Josh said.

"SILENCE," said Acting Superintendent Barkin. "Do not contradict me. If I say it is hard to tell them apart, it is hard to tell them apart."

"OK, Grandfather." Josh found the hammer. "Got any nails?"

"Do I *have* any nails?" said Acting Superintendent Barkin. "No. Gus will have some. You may ask him when we have fin-ished this conversation. So. Why have you come to visit me?"

"Um, I wanted to tell you that Miles put his lock on my jeans."

"Well, you have told me. Twice now. What do you want me to do about it?"

"I don't know. Maybe expel him? And Niles?"

Acting Superintendent Barkin shook his head. "Would that I could, Josh. Would that I could. I'm afraid a superintendent does not have the power to expel students. That is a principal's job. Your father would have to do it."

"Well that'll never happen!" Josh threw the hammer on the floor. "I think my dad *likes* Miles."

"I agree." Acting Superintendent Barkin smiled sadly. "Your father is hopeless. He is too full of the milk of human kindness."

Kindness. It was not the stuff of principals. And this was why Bertrand Barkin had become convinced that his son Principal Barkin had no business being a principal. Barry should be in a different line of work entirely, such as a vice principal.

Were he a vice principal, little Barry could ply his trade (such that it was) with all the kindness he cared to muster. He would fit in! As J. T. Solby, author of *The Seven Principles of Principal Power*, wrote in his follow-up leadership manual, *The Principal Vices of Vice Principals*, "kindness is a weakness common to today's vice principals, who would rather be applauded than obeyed." There was no room for the milk of human kindness in a good principal, who was already brimming with different dairy products altogether: the cream of command, the curds of cruelty, the whey of the master.

Bertrand Barkin watched his grandson, who was sullenly kicking the hammer. There was hope for Josh. The way he threw things (angrily) and kicked things (sullenly). The way he spoke (much too loudly). There was power in that boy. Yes. Sometimes complete dominance, like a cleft chin, skipped a generation. Looking at Josh, who was now trying to hammer the lock off his jeans, one thing was clear: The only milk in that boy was actual milk, from cows, which as you can imagine was a popular drink in Yawnee Valley.

"What's the point of being a dumb superintendent if you can't even get a couple of dumb nimbuses expelled?" Josh asked, hammering away.

"Patience, Josh. Patience. Power can take many forms, and

the power to expel is but one. Look around you. Look at the filing cabinets in the hallways. Look at these computers, which are new, or at least fairly new, purchased with that technology grant from a few years ago. These computers are plugged into databases a mere principal has no access to. Do you have any idea how much information flows through this building? Harriet Nervig Memorial Yawnee Valley District Office Building may as well be the center of the world. Here, I can wield power in its purest form. Knowledge."

Josh flinched from his grandfather, who was scary when he was shouting but terrifying when he spoke very softly.

"You want revenge on those two pranksters. So do I. I have

for many months now. But we will be patient. We will sit and listen and wait for our moment." Acting Superintendent Barkin walked over to his closet and removed what looked like a giant pair of pliers. "We will wait until the right tool presents itself to us. For the most powerful tool is the one that was made for the job."

Josh had been too distracted to catch much of his grandfather's speech. "What are those?" he asked.

"These? They are bolt cutters."

Every former principal kept a pair of bolt cutters around. At a school, locks had a way of ending up places they didn't belong: other people's lockers, chain link fences, the nets of basketball hoops . . . and now, his grandson. A little metal lock was no match for a former principal, let alone an Acting Superintendent.

"Hold still."

THAT NIGHT, around dinnertime, Stuart sat at the dinner table with his family, eating dinner. The meal was lasagna, Jeremy's specialty. Jeremy was Stuart's dad.

"So ANYWAY, that's why I need ANOTHER deodorant," Stuart said.

"You don't NEED deodorant in the FIRST place," said Jeremy. "You don't SWEAT yet."

"For you it's more like ODORANT," said Mary, Stuart's mom.

"I made that SAME JOKE at SCHOOL today!" said Stuart.

"Did everybody LAUGH?" asked Stuart's little sister, Annie.

"YES!" said Stuart. "They were DYING!"

"THAT'S our BOY," said Mary. "Always ready with a QUIP!"

"The CLASS CLOWN," said Stuart's dad. "JUST like his MOM."

"And his DAD," said Stuart's mom.

"And ME," said Annie, who had not started school yet.

"Well," said Jeremy, "it was very NICE of that MILES KID to stick up for you."

"AND the other one," said Mary.

"NILES," said Stuart. "They're my BEST friends. At SCHOOL, I mean. My BEST BEST friends are YOU GUYS."

"MILES and NILES," said Annie. "That's FUNNY."

She collapsed into hysterical tears.

"This JOSH character sounds ROTTEN," said Jeremy.

"He IS," said Stuart. "TRUST me, I've known him my WHOLE LIFE."

"Well, we'll get you another STICK of DEODORANT," said Mary.

"Or ODORANT," said Annie, repeating a joke that made everyone laugh even harder the second time.

"Maybe THIS TIME I should get AVALANCHE SCENT," said Stuart. "Since WATERFALL, you know, FELL! ON the GROUND!"

"You're so FUNNY, Chicken Stew!" said Mary, who sometimes called her son Chicken Stew as a joke.

The whole family collapsed into hysterical tears.

Six blocks away, at Original Yawnee Valley Pizza Parlor, Holly Rash and her father sat across from each other in what they called "their booth." A teenager wearing a white paper chef's hat delivered an extra-large pie with mushrooms, onions, and goat cheese. The Rashes gave it a few seconds to cool down. (They'd burnt the roofs of their mouths on pizza, more than once.)

"So," said Holly's dad, whose name was Dr. Rash but who didn't mind being called Bruce. "How was your day at school?"

Holly rolled her eyes. "C'mon, Dad!"

"What?"

"Ask something interesting. 'How was your day at school?' You can do better than that. It's a cliché."

"I wish I had never taught you that word."

"I would have learned it by now anyway."

"Well."

Judging from the steam coming off their pizza, their pie had cooled sufficiently. They each reached for a slice.

"Wait." He removed half a lemon from his pocket and smiled. "A little finishing touch."

"Did you bring that lemon from home, Dad?"

"Yes."

"In your pocket?

"Yes."

"What a dork!"

"Well, try it."

He squeezed the lemon over their slices. They both took bites, chewed thoughtfully, and washed them down with swigs of root beer.

"OK," said Holly. "This is really good. The best yet. The lemon pushes it to a 9.5."

"Looks like this dork is pret-ty cool," said Dr. Rash.

"Hmm," said Holly.

Mr. Rash pulled out a grease-stained notebook full of graph paper. "I am also going to give it a 9.5, thanks to the lemon I brought from home, but for the record, the reason I am not giving it a 10 is because the perfect pizza is not something you can taste on Earth but is an idea that exists only in God's mind."

He clicked a mechanical pencil and recorded their impressions. Every Monday night, Dr. Rash took Holly out to Original Yawnee Valley Pizza Parlor, just the two of them. Their goal was to try every possible combination of the restaurant's thirty-three offered toppings, in an effort to determine Yawnee

Valley's best pizza. Afterward, they went home and watched a movie together in the family room, and nobody was allowed to bother them. Originally, these outings with Dr. Rash were supposed to rotate among his three daughters, but now it was always him and Holly. Holly was Dr. Rash's favorite. Even though parents aren't supposed to have favorite children, many of them do. And in this case, even though everybody knew Dr. Rash liked Holly best, it was fine, since the other girls liked their mom better anyway (because of course kids have favorite parents too), and besides, nobody else in the family shared Dr. Rash's taste in movies.

Dr. Rash finished up his notes in their pizza journal and passed the notebook to Holly so she could make any necessary corrections and additions.

Dr. Rash waved the lemon. "Should I juice the whole thing?"

"Yes."

When he was finished, they each grabbed another slice.

"So you want an interesting question?" said Dr. Rash between bites. "OK. Well. How about this one."

Dr. Rash chewed a bit, then asked, "How's Niles Sparks?"

"Dad!"

✦ ✦ ✦

Somewhere in the distance, some cows ate their dinner, which was grass.

"Moo," said a cow that was green with purple spots, although you can't really tell in this picture.

The Barkins had pork chops.

Josh downed a glass of milk in one long gulp, which he considered one of his greatest talents. (He also considered it outrageous that last year Ms. Lewis, who ran the talent show, had not let him drink a glass of milk onstage and instead had given his slot to Janice Neeser, who rapped about cellular respiration. Some talent.)

Josh pounded his glass down on the table.

"Can I have some more?"

"Can I have some more *what?*" said Mrs. Barkin.

"Can I have some more *milk,*" said Josh. "Obviously."

"Your mother meant 'please,'" said Principal Barkin.

"I'm not talking to you," said Josh Barkin, to his father, which technically was talking to him.

"Josh, don't talk to your father that way," said Mrs. Barkin.

"Ugh! I'll just get it myself."

Josh stomped into the kitchen and returned with the whole gallon, which he slammed down next to his plate.

"Don't slam, Josh," said Principal Barkin.

"Don't slam *what?*" said Josh Barkin.

"Don't slam the milk," said Principal Barkin.

"I MEANT 'DON'T SLAM PLEASE!'" said Josh.

"Oh," said Mrs. Barkin.

"NOBODY RESPECTS ME AROUND HERE!" Josh took his pork chops and his milk gallon and stormed off to the living room. He threw himself onto the sofa and turned on the TV.

"Well." Mrs. Barkin speared a piece of pork on her fork.

"Well." Principal Barkin cut a roasted carrot in two.

They chewed their meat and vegetables, respectively, in silence. Well, not total silence—dings and buzzes came from the TV in the living room.

"Is that *Wheel of Fortune?*" Mrs. Barkin called out.

"Yeah," Josh said.

Mrs. Barkin loved *Wheel of Fortune*.

"What's the category?" she asked.

"Rhyme time," said Josh.

"Oh!" Mrs. Barkin brightened. "What's the puzzle?"

"A space F blank blank E N D space blank O space blank blank E space E N D."

Mrs. Barkin traced out the puzzle in the air with her index finger. "What was that, Joshy? A space F blank blank—"

"Oh, just go watch with him, Sharon," said Principal Barkin.

Alone at the table, Principal Barkin set to work on his chop.

These days, it was a pretty typical Barkin dinner.

So it was a pleasant surprise when the doorbell rang.

"NILES!" SAID PRINCIPAL BARKIN. "Miles! This is a pleasant surprise!" He checked his watch. "It's dinnertime, which normally is a bad time to go knocking on someone's door unannounced, but tonight, around here, it is a wonderful time to go knocking on my door, at least, unannounced!"

"We didn't knock," said Miles. "We rang the doorbell."

"Regardless!" said Principal Barkin. "Hello."

"Hey," said Miles.

"Hi," said Niles.

"So," said Principal Barkin. "Why are you here? Have you reconsidered my offer?"

"What offer?" said Miles.

"To flunk you!" said Principal Barkin. He corrected himself. "Or hold you back, rather. You know, that sounds harsh as well. We are in the business of raising students up, or at least pushing them forward. So let's just say, 'to have you two repeat a grade.' Yes. That's the word. Repeat. Think of it! You could repeat and repeat and repeat and repeat. You know that joke about Pete and Repete being in the boat, and then Pete falls out?"

"Yes," said Miles.

"It's kind of a dumb joke," said Niles.

"Yes. It would work better if people were actually named Repete. But that's not a name! You make an excellent point, Niles, and to be honest I never really liked that joke. But still! Our lives could be just like that joke. Repeat and repeat and repeat and repeat and repeat. Think of all the adventures we could have! Our capers could fill one hundred books! Like, what if the school board was going to close down Yawnee Valley Science and Letters Academy, but we saved the day with a giant prank?"

Niles frowned. "How would that work?"

"Aha! That's for you to figure out, Niles! Or how about this, a prank war with *another school?* Like St. Perpetua! A bunch of crazy pranks ahead of the Big Game!"

"What big game?" said Miles.

"A football game! Or basketball! Pick your sport!"

"But we don't play against St. Perpetua."

"We could, Miles! We could! And then at the end I could surprise everyone and do a huge slam dunk and win the Big Game at the buzzer! So I guess basketball."

"We don't want to flunk," said Niles.

"Ah," said Principal Barkin. "Then why are you here?"

"We need your help," said Miles.

"For a prank," said Niles.

Principal Barkin grinned. "Oh really!"

"Yes," said Miles and Niles, at the same time.

"What's the prank?" Principal Barkin asked.

"Well, Niles cooked it up," said Miles.

"We want to sneak into your dad's new office—"

"And you need my keys," said Principal Barkin. He shook his head sadly. "Let me stop you right there, boys. Even I, a principal, do not have the keys to the Harriet Nervig Memorial Yawnee Valley District Office Building. To get into my father's office, you need more than the help of a pranking principal. You would need, as a secret confederate, a pranking superintendent, and to my knowledge, a pranking superintendent is a thing that has never been, and a thing I cannot ever imagine existing."

"We don't need keys," said Miles.

"Don't be ridiculous, Miles. How else will we get in?"

"We *already have* the keys."

"ASTOUNDING!" said Principal Barkin. "WELL HOW DID YOU GET THEM?"

"From Gus," said Niles. "He cleans the district office too! We borrowed his keys today so we could dust the trophy case."

"I didn't even know we had a trophy case," said Principal Barkin.

"Well," said Niles, "I made an impression of the keys we'll need in a block of clay I got from the art room."

"And then after school we melted a bunch of pennies and poured the metal into the mold."

"It was like liquid metal Terminator!" said Miles, referring to a movie none of them had seen.

"That sounds dangerous," said Principal Barkin.

"I know what I'm doing," said Niles.

"He doesn't do *anything* until he knows what he's doing," said Miles.

"And your parents let you do this?"

"They don't really know what I do. They don't care."

"Oh. Ah. I don't know what to say to that," said Principal Barkin, which technically was saying something.

Niles shrugged. "Well, anyway, keys!"

Miles and Niles each held up a misshapen key and smiled at their principal.

"Will those work?"

"I think so," said Niles.

"I hope so," said Miles.

"But then," said Principal Barkin, "what do you need me for?"

Miles and Niles exchanged a look like *Here we go*.

"Principal Barkin," said Miles, "we need your *talent*."

Principal Barkin's eyes got very wide. "Go on. Please."

A FEW DAYS LATER, Acting Superintendent Barkin took a break from filling out a stack of forms to admire his own portrait.

He gasped. He started. He stood up straight.

"I don't remember any of this," he muttered, alone, in his office. Bertrand Barkin pressed his nose to the canvas. He wanted to get a better look at his tie. There was no doubt about it. Something was wrong. The tie was a foulard (yes, and Bertrand Barkin owned several foulards) with a red field (and all Bertrand's ties were red; it was the color of power), but the tie in this picture was decorated with a pattern of tiny violets. And Bertrand Barkin certainly did not own any ties with tiny violets on them! He owned a tie with tiny roses on it, red roses

on a red field, red on red, red squared, power to the second power! But violets? Never! In fact, reaching into his memory of the day he had sat for this portrait, Bertrand Barkin was certain that he had been wearing the tie with the roses. And, reaching into his memory of the many days he'd admired his own portrait, he felt somewhat but not totally certain that every time he'd looked at this painting, the tie in the picture had been covered in a spray of red blooms.

But now it had violets.

"Am I going mad?" he wondered, aloud, to himself, in the office. No. No! His mind was sharp. His vision, when he wore his glasses, was perfect. And so, Occam's razor (see *The Terrible Two Get Worse*, p. 65) would tell you that it must be that Bertrand Barkin had simply not noticed this before. That the artist had painted him in a tie with purple flowers. That it had been violets all along. Which was a comfort. And which was outrageous! Painters should paint only what exists in reality! None of this, what did they call it, artistic license. Artistic license was Bertrand Barkin's least favorite kind of license, worse than poetic license, worse even than a jet ski license.

Yes. Artistic license. That explained it.

Still, it was *strange*.

MORE TIME PASSED. More things happened. Quizzes were popped. The Nile River ran from south to north. When it started to snow, outdoor recesses were canceled. Indoors, at recess, Stuart went on a sixty-seven-game winning streak in Connect Four and declared himself "UNDEFEATABLE!" He lost the next game. Holly won the competitions on Ugly Sweater Day, '70s Day, and Dress Like a Teacher Day. (Scotty won Wacky Socks Day, but nobody really cared about Wacky Socks Day.) Josh made Stuart swallow a rock but didn't get caught. Several strange things were locked to Josh Barkin's pants: two padlocks, a bike lock, a bike. Ms. Shandy drew ziggurats on the blackboard, and triremes, and salt slabs, and various kinds of columns— Doric, Ionic, and Corinthian. "I don't remember any of this,"

Acting Superintendent Barkin
said in his office again

and again

and again.

The front office's bulletin board changed from turkeys to snowmen. Some of these things had never happened at school before, and some of them happened year after year. So many things happened, day after day, that it was easy for the kids in Miles and Niles's class to pretend that the days would last forever. But by the time the bulletin board went from hearts to shamrocks, the students found it impossible to forget that this year at this school was their last.

"I wonder if that's the last time Brendan is going to

fall out of his chair," Holly whispered to Niles after Brendan Burke, who liked to fall out of his chair to get attention in math class, fell out of his chair.

"I wonder if THIS is the LAST TIME they'll serve PEP-PERONI PIZZA," Stuart said in the cafeteria in late March. (It wasn't. They served pepperoni pizza every Friday and school didn't get out till May.) He dangled a pepperoni over his open mouth. "I better SAVOR IT."

"Josh," said Ms. Shandy on a lovely spring afternoon

when it seemed like the clock in her classroom just wouldn't strike three, "I hope this is the last time we will need to have this conversation."

And on that same afternoon, after the bell had finally rung, and Miles had gone to Niles's house, where they were both safely ensconced in the prank lab, Miles turned to Niles and said, "Hey. This is our last April Fools' Day."

"We'll still be here next year," Niles said. "We've got our whole lives full of April Fools' Days."

"I know," said Miles, "but our last April Fools' Day at *this* school."

"OK," said Niles. He picked up a piece of chalk and wrote 4/1 on the wall. "Let's do something funny then."

PRINCIPAL BARKIN was always the first person to arrive at Yawnee Valley Science and Letters Academy, but on April 1 he was even earlier than usual. He woke up at 4:44, one minute before his alarm went off, and hopped into the shower.

The water was cold, and Principal Barkin gave a little yelp. (The cold water was not a prank but the result of an unreliable hot water heater, which Principal Barkin insisted on fixing himself.) He pressed his back up against the tile, as far as he could get from the icy stream, and sang a little ditty to himself while he waited for the water to warm up.

Today's not just a school day!
Today is April Fools' Day!
A day-to-break-the-rules day!
Wow, so far this one rhymes!

Today's a prank-and-joke day!
A shake-your-can-of-Coke day!
But be careful with that Coke, hey!
It could spray in your eyes. Eye-ms.
It could spray in your eye-ms.
WAIT! NO! MERRY PRANKING TIMES!

It must have been the positive ions of the shower, or the negative ions of the shower—Principal Barkin was always hearing that the ions of the shower were good for your brain, but he could never remember whether the ions were positive or negative, and really he had no idea what an ion was— but anyway, mid-lather, Principal Barkin had an idea. For a prank. His first prank of April Fools' Day.

"Ha, ha!" he said in the shower. (He actually said ha, ha.)

When he had rinsed off, Principal Barkin wrapped a towel around himself and climbed up to the attic, where he found an old cardboard box labeled JOSH'S CREEPY CRAWLIES. He pulled out a rubber cobra (oh how little Josh had loved snakes!) and, returning to the bathroom, arranged the cobra in a threatening pose on the floor of the tub.

"Sharon is going to love this!" Principal Barkin said.

He chuckled.

Then he stopped chuckling.

"Actually, Sharon might not love this," he said.

After some reflection, Principal Barkin decided that Sharon would probably not love it, and removed the rubber snake from the tub. But halfway up the ladder to return the cobra to its box, Principal Barkin said, "Oh what the hey! It's April Fools' Day!" And he scampered back to the bathroom with the snake.

"Ha, ha!" he said. The second time around, the coil was even more threatening.

At the breakfast table, spreading oatmeal on his toast, Principal Barkin had another idea. "Is this whole house full of ions this morning?" he wondered. He fetched Josh's box of sugar cereal from the pantry, removed the plastic bag—with all its marshmallows and sprinkle-spangled clusters— and replaced it with a bag of Mrs. Barkin's flax and fiber flakes. "Ha, ha!" said Principal Barkin, hiding the bag of sugar cereal under the sink, behind some sponges. "Josh may or may not love this, and in fact probably will not, but what the hey, what the hey!"

And it was with great pep that Principal Barkin stepped out to his car and sped off to school.

His office was seriously lacking in ions. All week he'd been cooping himself up in there, trying to fulfill his principal duties while also cooking up a delicious April Fools' joke to play on Miles and Niles. And he had nothing to show for it. So this morning he reported straight to his secret hideout, a shelter from the school's hurly-burly, the hermitage where he could sit in solitude and do his best thinking: the utility closet on the second floor.

But even there he could not relax. The mops smelled musty. His favorite bucket to sit on was missing—he must ask Gus about that missing bucket—and he had to sit on a different bucket. And make no mistake—this new bucket, as a seat, was inferior. Plus, his wristwatch kept ticking, which was infuriating. "Is it just me, or is this watch louder today?" Usually he didn't notice his watch ticking at all, but this morning he could not stop noticing it. "Confound you, time!" Principal Barkin scolded his watch and was in the middle of removing it from his wrist and placing it under a bucket when he noticed that it was 5:45, and he had to unlock the doors for Janice Neeser, who got to school early on Fridays because her mom had to get to work all the way over in Cherry Valley. "Confound you, Janice Neeser!" Barkin said, then immediately felt bad for saying it.

He rushed downstairs—it was a brisk April morning, and he didn't want to leave Janice out there in the cold—and sure enough, there was Janice, hands cupped around her eyes, face pressed against the glass of the front door.

"Sorry, sorry! Be right there, Janice!" Principal Barkin jogged down the hallway and fumbled for his keys. "Which one, which one, ah, here we go!"

Principal Barkin opened the front door.

"Sorry, good morning, and ah!" said Principal Barkin. "Janice, what on earth is that?"

"A giant schnoodle," said Janice Neeser.

"A what?" said Principal Barkin.

"A cross between a giant schnauzer and a poodle. A giant schnoodle."

"Well, clearly that is something you just made up, but obviously it is some sort of dog."

"His name is Horatio," said Janice Neeser.

"And dogs," Principal Barkin continued, "are not allowed at school, unless Horatio is a service dog, in which case, of course, he is welcome at school. Is he a service dog?"

"No."

"Then he is not welcome at school. You will have to take him home."

"My mom already left," said Janice Neeser.

"Yes. Well. That is not my problem." But as soon as he said it, Principal Barkin realized that this *was* his problem. "I'll tell you what, Janice, we will go find a blanket, which we will place in my car, and I will drive Horatio to my house, where he can stay for the—oh. My wife, Mrs. Barkin, is allergic to dogs."

"Giant schnoodles are hypoallergenic!" said Janice Neeser.

"I do not understand anything you just said," said Principal Barkin.

"They don't shed!" said Janice Neeser.

"I see," said Principal Barkin. "That solves one problem, but I am just now thinking of another problem, which is that my wife, Mrs. Barkin, hates dogs."

Janice gasped. She covered her dog's ears with her hands. "Don't listen, Horatio!" she said in a voice she used only for Horatio.

"I'll tell you what. Horatio can spend the day in the utility closet until your mom can come get him."

"Gross! Horatio doesn't want to live in the utility closet."

"I assure you it's very pleasant."

"No!" She rubbed Horatio's head. "You don't want to hide in a nasty closet, do you, Horatio, do you?" she said in that voice again.

Watching Janice Neeser talk to her dog on a dark, cold morning, it finally occurred to Principal Barkin to ask a question he should have asked much earlier.

"Janice, why did you bring your dog to school?"

"Because it's Bring Your Pet to School Day!"

"What?"

"It's Bring Your Pet to School Day! The flyers got passed around last week!"

"What flyers?"

"The flyers that said to bring your pets to school!"

"Janice, today is not Bring Your Pet to School Day. Yawnee Valley Science and Letters Academy does not have a Bring Your Pet to School Day. Today is a special day, but it is April Fools'—oh, I see what's happening."

"The sign out front even *says* it!"

"Oh dear." What could he do? A phone tree? A phone tree! If he called two parents, and they called two parents, and they called two parents. He checked his watch. Confound you, time! No, even a phone tree couldn't save him now. "What am I going to do?"

WELL, what could he do?

Chapter
26

H^e laughed.

"WELL PLAYED, boys, well played."

Principal Barkin reclined in his desk chair and examined a flyer for Bring Your Pet to School Day. "This looks real."

"Thanks!" said Miles.

"Can I keep this?"

"Sure," said Niles. (He had already set aside a copy to go in his scrapbook and, eventually, in his planned pranking museum.)

"Thank you," said Principal Barkin. He pulled open his bottom desk drawer and a dove flew out.

"What the hey?" Principal Barkin said as the dove flapped wildly in the airspace around his head before settling on his desk. "How did that get in there?"

(Masterstroke.)

"I think that's Stephanie Spitoleri's," said Niles, coaxing the bird into his hands and cradling it under the jacket of his suit. "We can bring it back to her. She's in our science class."

"Wonderful," said Principal Barkin. "That would be wonderful. I must say, prankster-to-pranksters, this was a very impressive prank. A terrific prank. In fact, I invited you to my office not just to hang out and chew the fat like a bunch of pranksters, but also to celebrate your achievement, as well as this wonderful day."

He carefully opened his second desk drawer, in case there was an animal hiding in it.

(There wasn't.)

"Wonderful," said Principal Barkin. He produced a plastic tray loaded with Oreos. "An April Fools' Day feast,"  he said with a wink. He picked up a cookie. "Dig in, boys!"

"Did you replace the cream with toothpaste?" Niles asked.

Principal Barkin's face fell. "How did you know?"

Niles shrugged. "It's sort of a . . ."

"Classic?" Miles said.

"Yeah, classic." (The word Niles had been thinking of was "cliché.")

"Plus you winked," said Miles.

"Ah. Right. The winking."

He broke the cookie in his hand into three pieces. "Well, we can share this one, then. I didn't do anything to it. It's the one I was going to eat."

The three of them each had a third of an Oreo.

Principal Barkin took out two cans of Coke from the drawer.

"We're not supposed to have soda at school, but who wants a Coke!"

"Did you shake them?" Niles asked.

Principal Barkin put the cans of Coke back in his desk drawer.

"I didn't even wink!"

"Another classic," said Niles.

"Niles, you are being kind, but I hear you, loud and clear. I need to be more original, like you two. In fact, since you won't be here next year, do you mind if I steal your Pet Day prank from you?"

"What do you mean?" said Niles.

"Can I use your prank when you're gone?"

"Principal Barkin," said Niles, "you're the principal. If you say it's Bring Your Pet to School Day, it wouldn't be a prank. It would just be Bring Your Pet to School Day."

"Oh blah!" Principal Barkin slammed his fist on his desktop, startling Stephanie Spitoleri's dove. "It's so hard to prank when you're powerful!"

"Well you could do it anyway," said Miles. "Just declare a Bring Your Pet to School Day. That might be fun."

Principal Barkin considered that. "That might be fun, Miles. It might. And so maybe I will! Assuming nobody gets bitten today."

And luckily nobody did.

ACTING SUPERINTENDENT Barkin strode down the first-floor hallway of Yawnee Valley Science and Letters Academy. It was a passing period, so the hallway was full of students, which was normal, and animals, which was not normal. His only reaction, passing dogs, cats, snakes, ferrets, iguanas, pigs, and children, was to wrinkle his nose a tiny bit. He was not here to insist the children's pets be quarantined until 3:00 P.M., although he certainly had the power to do so. He was not here to berate his son for his failures as a principal, although this corridor, teeming with pets, was certainly cause for a good berating. No, Acting Superintendent Bertrand Barkin did not care one whit about the chaos in the hallway, which was unusual. Because he hated chaos. On an ordinary day, Acting Superintendent Barkin, hearing about this ridiculous pet prank, would have rushed to Yawnee Valley Science and Letters Academy and quickly restored order. But this was not an ordinary day. Bertrand Barkin was not here for order. He was here for revenge.

He found Miles and Niles by the science lab.

"Hello." Acting Superintendent Barkin loomed over the boys. He was an excellent loomer. As a young man, he'd spent hours practicing in the mirror, looming over houseplants, floor lamps, trash cans—anything roughly the height of a child. He gestured toward the menagerie parading through the hallway. "I suppose all this is your work."

"We don't know what you're talking about," said Miles Murphy, who was an excellent denier.

"Of course not." Bertrand Barkin sighed. "It's quite a prank you've pulled off here. A real spectacle. I daresay a victory." He held up his hands and chuckled. "I surrender!"

This was weird.

Miles and Niles did not say anything.

"You and your little buddy here are unstoppable. I'm just glad I won't have to deal with you next year."

Niles couldn't resist. "Don't worry, Acting Superintendent Barkin! Since you're in charge of all the schools in the district now, I'm sure we'll have plenty of opportunities to run into each other!"

Bertrand Barkin's eyes clapped on Niles. "I wasn't speaking to you," he hissed. "I was speaking to Niles."

"I am Niles," said Niles.

"Oh, you know who I mean! Him! Miles!"

"OK," said Miles. "Well, I'll still be here too."

Old Man Barkin's face assumed an expression of mock sympathy, an expression he'd also practiced in the mirror. (Sympathy was a weakness in powerful people, but *mock* sympathy had its uses.) "Oh," he said. "You don't know."

"Don't know what?" Miles said.

Acting Superintendent Barkin waved his hands. "I shouldn't say. In fact, I've already said too much."

"You haven't said anything." Miles's voice was rising. And Niles was getting an unpleasant tickle in his stomach.

"It's really not my news to deliver," said Acting Superintendent Barkin.

"What news?" Miles almost shouted. "What are you talking about?"

"You should ask your mother tonight. I've obviously spoken too soon. I know communication sometimes suffers in broken homes."

Miles was furious. He hated that term, "broken home." And he felt sure that Acting Superintendent Barkin somehow knew he hated that term, so he tried not to react. But he could feel his face getting hot. Miles felt like he was being swept up by a net, that he had triggered a booby trap and would soon be dangling from a tree.

"Perhaps my mistake is for the best," said Bertrand Barkin. "Perhaps the news is better coming from me, an authority figure, someone you respect."

Miles stood still.

Niles had a far-off expression.

"Miles," said Acting Superintendent Barkin, "your mother called the district office this morning. I had the pleasure of speaking to her. She requested one of these."

He removed a neatly folded piece of paper from a pocket of his blazer and showed it to Miles.

"Do you know what this is?"

"It's . . . a form?"

"Indeed it is. A transcript request form. And this one has your name on it."

He checked the form to make sure he had the name right. "Miles Murphy."

Miles swallowed. "OK."

"This job, my job, involves many forms. And every form has a different purpose. A transcript request form is used to obtain a copy of your student file, your report cards and such. She needed to send your grades to a new school. In another state. You're moving this summer."

Miles and Niles stared at Old Man Barkin.

They waited for his thin lips to curl into a cruel smile, for him to open his mouth and say, "April Fools."

But the old man just shook his head

and said, "I'm sorry. I thought you already knew."

Acting Superintendent Barkin closed his eyes and inhaled. The universe, all on its own, was by turns cruel and kind. But a certain kind of person—a patient person, a perceptive person, a *powerful* person—could amplify the natural energy of the universe. A powerful person could at certain moments, through some effort, make the universe's cruelties just a little bit crueler. (Bertrand Barkin supposed one might also have the power to make the universe's kindnesses kinder, but kindness had never been his métier.) Did Bertrand Barkin make Miles Murphy move? Of course not. The universe did that. And that was bad. But not bad enough. For Miles to learn of that move like this, from his old nemesis, in the afterglow of a successful April Fools' Day prank committed with his best friend—well, that was truly awful. Bertrand Barkin took in this moment. His moment. He looked at Miles, and then at Niles, or perhaps it was the other way around. This business with the names was ridiculous. But Bertrand Barkin looked at them both. He relished the looks on their faces, the instant they realized their inane little club, the Terrible Two, would be torn asunder. It was delicious.

"Nothing lasts forever, boys," he said.

Then he turned and left. He had more forms to fill out and more people's days to ruin. He was a very busy man.

Josh Barkin, who'd been alerted ahead of time, appeared in the doorway of the science lab and smirked. "Sorry, nimbuses."

This couldn't be right.

This was wrong.

Miles Murphy ran down the halls, through the front doors, down the road, away from his school.

Chapter 29

MILES MURPHY couldn't think. His brain was buzzing, but he didn't need to think. He knew the way by heart. He knew all the roads in Yawnee Valley by heart. He had this whole town memorized. Numb, buzzing, he sprinted down Sunnyslope Road, to Trellis Drive, to Hawk Street, which turned into Raven Way and spilled onto Railroad Avenue. Left on Milkpail Place, a shortcut, past the golf course, right on Signal Street, right on Main Street, up the steps and through the door of the Yawnee Valley Post Office, which was where Miles's mom worked.

There was a line.

(There was always a line in the afternoons.)

Miles waited.

Slowly, the line moved. Miles shuffled forward. He tried getting his mother's attention, but like most people who worked in places with long lines, Judy Murphy never looked at the people queued up for her window, because they were almost always looking back at her with impatient and annoyed expressions. Miles Murphy was five back in line. "Next," said Judy Murphy. And then, four minutes later, "Next."

At last, Miles reached the front of the line. He played absentmindedly with the plastic clip that held the vinyl line divider to a plastic post. He could hear his mom helping a customer.

"So you're saying I could use this stamp to mail a letter in the year 3030," said a gray-haired man in overalls.

"Yes," said Judy Murphy. "It's a forever stamp. That means it will be sufficient postage for a first-class letter not weighing over one ounce, forever."

"I probably won't be alive in the year 3030," said the man.

"You never know, sir," said Judy Murphy.

"But I could leave this stamp to my great-great-grand-children, and they could mail a letter with it," said the man.

"Correct," said Judy Murphy. She was very patient.

"Probably won't even be letters then. Probably won't be mail. We'll just teleport stuff."

"Well, I love the mail," said Judy Murphy. "And I can't predict the future, but I think the mail will be around for a long time."

"This stamp would be good in the year 12,000, is what you're saying."

"Forever."

"That's 10,000 years from now. What if there's no United States of America by then?

Miles couldn't believe this.

"What if we're ruled by space aliens?" asked the man. "Are the space aliens going to honor this stamp?"

"As long as the United States exists, you'll be able to mail a letter with this stamp."

"Aha!" said the man. "So it's not forever! False advertising!"

A woman in a blue uniform came and opened the window next to Judy's. (Her name was Eileen, and she'd just come back from lunch.)

"Next," said Eileen.

"Uh," said Miles. He didn't know what to do. A woman behind him sighed, a man cleared his throat, and Miles stepped uncertainly to Eileen's window.

"I'm here to see my mom," Miles said.

"Your mom?" said Eileen.

Judy recognized her son's voice and looked over.

"Miles! What are you doing here? Why aren't you in school?"

"Oh! You're Miles!" said Eileen. "It's nice to finally meet you, Miles. I've heard a lot about you. Judy, I can help your customer. Sir, I can help you."

"Thank you," said the gray-haired man, shouldering Miles out of the way. "So eventually, in billions of years, the universe is going to stop expanding, is one theory."

He and Eileen commenced a long conversation that won't be recorded in this novel.

"Mom," said Miles, "are we moving again?"

"What?" said Judy.

"Are we moving again?"

Her expression said yes first. And then she did.

"Yes."

Chapter 30

JUDY MURPHY took her lunch break early, shut down her station, and walked with Miles to Applesauce Park. (The park was not named for the food, applesauce, but for a cow, Applesauce, who had accidentally been elected mayor of Yawnee Valley in 1836 and then reelected on purpose four years later.)

Judy and Miles sat beneath the statue of Applesauce and shared a sandwich. They had both been crying, but they were finished, for now at least.

"Why didn't you tell me?" said Miles.

"I was going to tell you. I was figuring out how to tell you." Suddenly Judy Murphy became angry, but not at Miles. "Why did your principal tell you?"

"It wasn't Principal Barkin. It was his dad, Former Principal Barkin."

"Well that's confusing," said Judy.

"Not for me," said Miles.

"Well anyway, it was none of his business. And he said 'broken home'? What a terrible man!"

(She was right about that.)

"I should complain," said Judy Murphy.

"You'd just be complaining to him," said Miles. "He's in charge of everything. Plus he'll say it was just an accident."

"But I told him I hadn't told you yet."

"Yeah."

"But why would he tell you? Why, if I said I hadn't told you?"

"Mom," said Miles, "that's *why* he told me."

"I can't believe there are people like that in this world," Judy said.

(But there are.)

"What a terrible man!" Judy said.

(Yes.)

"I don't want to move," said Miles.

He'd already said this a lot that afternoon, in the park.

"I know," said Judy.

"We already moved," said Miles. "Two years ago. We moved here. Why do we have to keep moving?"

"I got another job, Miles. A much better job."

She'd already said this a lot too.

"It pays a lot more," Judy said. "We'll have a lot more money. Things will be better."

"That's what you said when we moved here."

"And things did get better!"

"Yeah, so they already got better. They can't just keep getting better. Things will get worse."

"They won't be worse."

"Promise?"

Judy Murphy took a bite of her sandwich. "I can't promise that. But I hope they will get better."

"This is so stupid. This is stupid, stupid, stupid."

"Miles."

"This is not how my life was supposed to go."

"It's our life, Miles."

"You can't just make decisions for me!"

"I can. I'm your mom. I'm trying to do what's best for us!"

"You're wrong!"

"Miles."

"My best friend lives here."

"You can still keep in touch with Niles. You kept in touch with Carl and Ben."

"No I didn't! I haven't talked to those guys in over a year!"

"Well, I'm sure it will be different with Niles."

"How do you know? You don't know anything!"

"Miles."

"You can't just come and change my whole life out of the blue like this!"

(But of course whole lives *can* change this way, all of a sudden. They often do.)

"Miles."

"Don't I get any say? Doesn't anyone care what I think?"

"I care."

(She did.)

"But we're still moving."

"Yes."

"This isn't fair!"

(It wasn't.)

"I know that."

(She did.)

Judy Murphy looked at her son. He wiped his eyes.

"I'm so sorry, Miles," she said.

(She was.)

AT HALF PAST THREE Miles let himself into the house at 47 Buttercream Lane (the Sparkses never locked their front door) and found Niles lying on the floor of the prank lab, listening to music, staring at the ceiling.

"Hey," said Niles.

"Hey," said Miles. "Are they mad I ran out of school?"

"Nobody's mad, but they're going to make you serve detention."

"Oh," said Miles. "OK."

"I'll serve it with you," Niles said.

Miles smiled. "Cool."

Miles stood there in the prank lab, its four walls covered with plans for future pranks and pranks recently played, written on top of half-erased blueprints from pranks long past.

"It's true, huh?" Niles said. "You're moving again. It's real."

"Yeah," said Miles. "It's real."

"When?"

"Summer. What is this music?"

It barely sounded like music. People were counting and chatting while a pipe organ played long, low, slowly blooming notes. It sounded like math.

"It's an opera about Einstein," said Niles.

"Oh. How long is it?"

"Three and a half hours."

"OK."

Miles got down on the floor next to Niles. They lay there and listened till about seven. By then they were both hungry, so Niles made some spaghetti and meatballs.

It was the start of a conversation—The Conversation—that stretched over the next few weeks. What began in the prank lab continued, off and on, starting up with absolutely no warning and abandoned just as quickly. Niles would be in the middle of explaining why tic-tac-toe was a bad game. "If both players know what they're doing, it'll always end in a tie." Miles needed to see the problem drawn out, and while Niles was making a bunch of grids on a piece of paper, Miles said, "We can still write to each other, right?"

Niles didn't even look up from the drawings. "Yeah, of course. See, the player who makes the first move should always choose the center square. Then player two . . ."

Then a few days later, in detention, when Coach O. wasn't looking, Niles slipped Miles an origami envelope made from a piece of loose-leaf paper. Inside there was a book of stamps.

The next week, they were making up the rules for a new version of Monopoly, one that would take even *longer*, and Niles said, "Plus we can do regular phone calls too."

"Yeah," said Miles. "I mean calls are basically free, right?"

"Yeah," said Niles. "I think so."

Then he wrote down RULE 83: IF THE DOG LANDS ON THE SAME SQUARE AS THE BOOT, IT CAN EAT THE BOOT.

Miles looked over Niles's shoulder and nodded. "I think we could actually make a lot of money off this. Like we could sell it to Hasbro."

"I agree," said Niles.

In those last weeks before summer, most of the time it would be like Miles was never leaving, and then, suddenly, it would become very clear that he was. One second they would be writing in the prank lab or releasing ladybugs in Miles's mom's garden. And then, one of them would suddenly, inevitably continue The Conversation.

One day they were taking a walk in the woods, past a grand old sycamore in which they'd once built (and destroyed) a tree house, when Niles said, "You know you're going to be OK, right?"

They stopped under the tree.

"What do you mean?" Miles asked.

"You're going to be fine. You know how to do this. You already did it once. You're good at moving."

"What does that mean? How can somebody be good at moving?"

Niles shrugged. "You're good at making friends. That's the only thing to be worried about, and you shouldn't be worried. You had friends in your old town. And then we're friends here."

"You're my best friend," Miles said.

"Yeah. Obviously. You're my best friend too. But before you came to Yawnee Valley, I didn't have any friends. Really. Like zero."

Miles didn't disagree, because he knew that was true.

Niles was perfectly matter-of-fact. "I'm terrible at making friends. I think it's me we should be worried about."

Miles was stunned. Since he'd found out he was moving, it hadn't occurred to him that he should worry about Niles. It wasn't that Miles was being selfish. Maybe it was a little bit that Miles was being selfish. But mostly it was this: Miles Murphy *never* worried about Niles Sparks. Because Niles always seemed to have things figured out. Niles thought about everything. Niles always had a plan. Niles was always right. Right?

Normally Miles would let The Conversation drop here, think about what Niles had just said, and bring it up again later, when he'd figured out what to say. But something about Niles's face, this face:

told Miles that he'd better say something now. So Miles opened his mouth without knowing what was going to come out of it.

"Niles, you're wrong."

Niles frowned. "I don't think so."

"No, you are. You're wrong."

"Hmmm," said Niles.

"I mean, you're right that you're terrible at making friends."

Niles winced.

"But!" said Miles. "You're really good at *being* friends. Like amazing. You're great at it. And you can trust me. Because I've had a lot of friends."

Niles's face had changed a little, and for the better, but Miles knew he had better keep going.

"And it's fine if you're terrible at making friends, because while I was here, we made friends, I mean, we made *other* friends, together."

"What do you mean?"

"I mean like Holly. And Stuart!"

Niles blushed. "You think Holly's my friend?"

"Obviously! You guys spent the whole summer hanging out together, when you weren't hanging out with me."

"Yeah, but that feels different. It feels different than you and me."

"Every friendship feels different! That's how it works with friendships. It's you and another person. It's different every time!"

"Huh," said Niles. "And you think we're friends with Stuart?"

"I *know* we're friends with Stuart."

"Wow."

"I know. I'm surprised too. And you'll keep being friends with them after I'm gone. And it won't be the same, and probably in a lot of ways it will be worse. But maybe in some ways it will be better." (And even though Miles said that, he preferred not to think about it.) "Look, this whole thing is awful, everything is awful, and it's horrible, but you're going to be OK, and I'm going to be OK. We're both going to be OK. OK?"

Niles smiled.

"OK."

IN THESE LAST WEEKS of board games and walks in the woods, of solemn discussions about moving and friendship, you might be wondering: As the end of the school year approached, did Miles and Niles talk about pranking?

Well, no.

And since you may have come to expect that this book, this whole series, was about a couple of *pranksters*, you would be forgiven for asking: Hey, what gives?

Had sadness crushed our heroes' spirits? Had Bertrand Barkin's rotten-hearted connivances extinguished the mischievous flicker in Miles's and Niles's souls? Was that Pet Day prank the Terrible Two's last practical joke? Is the whole rest of this book going to be sad conversations in the woods?

No way. Of course not. This is Miles Murphy and Niles Sparks we're talking about here.

So: Let's talk a little bit more about Miles. The truth is, on the same day he had learned of his imminent departure from Yawnee Valley, after he had run to the post office and listened to a very long, very strange opera with Niles, Miles Murphy had gone home, shut himself in his room, and pulled out his pranking notebook. He flipped past blueprints and lists, plans and schemes, chaos and nightmares and confusion, until he found a blank page. He wrote

You see, up in the prank lab, somewhere around hour two of that opera, Miles Murphy had a realization. An epiphany. Niles had years and years of pranks in Yawnee Valley ahead of him. But Miles? Miles needed to leave his mark. Miles Murphy had lived in this town for more than two years, a

significant chunk of his life so far, and if he had to leave this place, he wanted to be sure he left Yawnee Valley changed.

Every night, long after his mother had gone to sleep, Miles would pad around his room in his nightshirt, thinking. He added ideas to his list.

After a week of what Mr. Maxwell, his English teacher, called "Blue-Sky Brainstorming" (a very confusing term), Miles revisited his list. He crossed out any ideas that seemed impossible, impractical, unimpressive, or unappealing.

He threw the notebook against the wall.

Then he did it all again.

Weeks went by and Miles still had no plan. His notebook was pretty busted up from being thrown against the wall so many times. And he began to become convinced that he would never think of anything good at all.

Maybe he would have to ask Niles for help.

But Miles did not want to ask Niles for help.

Because although he was sure that Niles could help him, that Niles would come up with a great idea, Miles wanted to do this himself. It was his last prank! And he had a feeling that Niles understood this, because not once since April Fools' Day had Niles brought up any kind of final prank. Miles knew Niles had noticed him scribbling in his notebook one time during Ms. Shandy's class and another time, after school, when Miles was sitting on the sofa and Niles was beating the final boss on his favorite video game. Niles noticed everything. And Niles understood. Niles was a person who sometimes needed to be left alone, who disappeared into his own brain. Miles had learned to give his friend the space he needed. Now he was grateful that Niles knew how to give him some space too.

It was the night of the day of the conversation under the

sycamore that Miles finally figured it out. (This was not a co-incidence.) It was almost midnight. He was pacing in his underwear. (No nightshirt. It was a warm night. Summer was coming.) He was whistling a song he knew well, softly, so he wouldn't wake up his mom. Miles often whistled while he walked around, thinking. When he came to the end of this particular tune, he added a few notes of his own. This was also something Miles did often—you already know this. Miles was a gifted whistler. He whistled without thinking. But that night Miles startled himself. He heard himself whistling. Those three simple notes Miles had added himself were so pretty that he had to stop pacing.

Miles Murphy realized he'd been going about this last prank all wrong.

He found another blank page in his notebook and wrote

THE NEXT MORNING found Miles Murphy downtown, in Yawnee Valley Jewelers. (Not for a diamond heist. Unfortunately.)

"How long will it take?" he asked the shopkeeper.

She looked at a calendar by the register. "How about next Thursday."

Friday was the Good-bye Grads School Dance.

"That's perfect," Miles said.

The shopkeeper handed Miles a form to fill out, and when

he was finished, she checked it over. "Your name's Niles?" she asked.

"No, I'm Miles."

She looked closer at the paper. "Oh! Right. Wow, I see. That's funny."

"What's funny about that?" Miles asked.

"Nothing." The shopkeeper gave Miles an odd smile. "Nothing."

"Hmmm," Miles said.

A little bell rang when Miles walked out the door. It was Saturday, so Miles went to the doughnut shop, where, amid farmers reading newspapers and drinking coffee, Niles had already managed to find them a table.

"Hey." Miles sat down. It was exciting, having a secret from his friend.

"Hey." Niles looked up. He had a secret too.

THE GOOD-BYE GRADS SCHOOL DANCE was an annual tradition, a dance (the only dance Yawnee Valley Science and Letters Academy hosted) replete with a DJ, crepe paper, tinsel, a disco ball, and snacks. It took place at 4:00 P.M. in the gymnasium. To create ambience, Gus had taped up black construction paper against all the windows. The strong afternoon sunlight still managed to bleed through, making the paper glow gold at the edges, but as long as you didn't look up at the windows, it kind of felt like evening. The dance was a real event.

For once, Niles wasn't the only one in a suit. Kids brought fancy clothes from home and changed in the locker room after the three o'clock bell. (Niles tied Miles's tie for him.) Then students gathered in the hall and milled around while, inside the gym, the DJ set up giant speakers and the teachers laid out treats they'd baked at home. At four on the dot, the doors swung open. Principal Barkin welcomed the kids.

"CONGRADULATIONS!" he said. "I DON'T KNOW IF YOU COULD HEAR THAT, BUT I WAS SAYING CONGRADULATIONS, WITH A *D* AS IN GRADS! LIKE GRADUATES!" The music began. Heavy bass shook the gym's metal risers. Kids streamed inside and took up places around the edges of the room, their backs against the tumbling mats that were velcroed to the wall. Boys were on one side of the room, girls on the other. Everybody stared at each other. Three songs played, and nobody danced, except the DJ, a student at Yawnee Valley Agricultural College, who was bouncing around in his booth and seemed to be at a different, much better party.

Four more songs played. Nobody danced. But there was some commotion at the snack table over Ms. Shandy's blondies, after word of their deliciousness somehow made it around the gym.

"These are really good," Miles said with his mouth full, safely back against the wall.

"It's the chips," said Niles. "Are these vanilla chips?"

"ENOUGH is ENOUGH!" said Stuart. "SOMEBODY'S got to get this PARTY STARTED. HOLD my BLONDIE."

Stuart handed Niles a napkin wrapped around a half-eaten treat and strode onto the empty basketball court. There, alone, he began to dance, somehow using only his arms.

"Whoa," said Miles.

"Wow," said Niles.

Soon some teachers joined Stuart on the dance floor. Mr. Gebott and Ms. Machle partnered up. They did a lot of twirls and spins and dips. It was an old-fashioned dance that looked funny when such a new song was playing. Ms. Shandy partnered up with Stuart and tried to show him how to shift his legs with the beat.

"THANKS, Ms. Shandy, but I have MY OWN style!"

Eventually, kids crossed the room, walked up alone to groups of friends, swallowed hard, and asked each other to dance. The answer was always yes. The court filled up, and the music got louder.

"I'm going to the bathroom," said Miles.

"I'm going to get another blondie," said Niles.

Miles walked off, but not toward the bathrooms.

Niles walked off, but not toward the blondies.

(The blondies were long gone anyway.)

Miles ducked underneath the bleachers and hunched along in the darkness. He didn't want to crawl and get dust on his suit. Invisible to the nearby revelers, he crossed the whole length of the gym. Coach B. and Coach O. were standing by the exit.

Miles needed to get through that door.

He stood there, breathing hard.

Could he sneak behind them?

Throw a smoke bomb and create a distraction?

That would work, but he did not have any smoke bombs.

And it didn't seem like these guys were going anywhere.

"I'm just saying that diet and mood are related, Tom," said Coach B. "And excuse my honesty but you've been crabby for pretty much the last two years."

"Crabby?" said Coach O. "Mike, I'm a paragon of the low-carb *lifestyle*, and if you can't support me on my

journey—whoa whoa whoa, Janice!" He began blowing his whistle.

"Hey!" Coach B. blew his whistle. "Scotty!"

They rushed to the dance floor.

Silently thanking Scotty and Janice for their inappropriate dancing, Miles sprinted out the door and into the hallway. He quietly shut the doors behind him. The music in the gym sounded far-off and muddy. Miles reached into the pocket of his suit jacket and pulled out a tiny screwdriver. Then he tiptoed over to the trophy case.

Niles was already there, kneeling, staring perplexedly at his very large key ring.

"What are you doing here?" Miles asked.

Niles looked up, surprised. "What are you doing here?"

"Pranking," they both said, at the same time.

Niles tossed his key ring on the floor and pulled out a

tiny screwdriver. "Want to help me? Know how to jimmy a lock?"

Then he noticed Miles already had a screwdriver in his hand.

"Wait," said Niles.

Miles smiled. He pulled a key from his coat. "Are you looking for this?"

Niles stared at the key in Miles's hand. "Where did you get that?"

"I stole it off your key chain."

"When?"

"Three days ago."

Niles thought back. "When you forgot your hat in my room?"

"Yeah. I left it there on purpose."

"Nice."

It was beginning to dawn on both of them what was now happening, or what might now be happening, or at least what they hoped was now happening.

"What's your prank?" Niles asked.

"What's *your* prank?" Miles asked.

"I don't want to say," Niles said. "Just in case."

"Well *I'm* not going first," Miles said.

"OK," said Niles. "Let me ask this: Is there something else in your pocket?"

Miles smiled. "Yes."

Niles smiled. "Does it fit in the palm of your hand?"

"Yes."

"Count of three?"

They each reached into their coat pockets and brought out a closed fist.

"One," said Miles.

"Two," said Niles.

"Three," they both said, at the same time.

Their fingers unfolded and they held their hands out to each other.

Miles's hands were bigger than Niles's, but they were each holding a small brass plaque.

MILES
NILES'S BEST FRIEND

NILES
MILES'S BEST FRIEND

Miles's and Niles's smiles widened.

"What are the chances," said Niles.

"I don't even believe it," said Miles.

"I do," said Niles.

"Yeah, me too," said Miles.

In the years to come, Miles Murphy would have many more ideas for pranks. Extraordinary pranks, brilliant pranks, colossal pranks that were baroque and sometimes very expensive. But his favorite idea, the one he would always be proudest of, was the one he thought of with Niles Sparks, together, separately.

It took no more than a minute to replace the plaques on Bertrand Barkin's second-place trophy.

Miles locked up the cabinet. Then they each held up two fingers and touched their fingertips together.

And Miles and Niles gave each other a look that said *We will be friends for the rest of our lives.* And they would. Of course they would. Because Miles and Niles were real friends, and real friendship is something that lasts forever.

"So be it," they said softly, at the same time.

"So this is how it ends!" Principal Barkin was standing a few feet away, holding a large gold picture frame. "Not with a bang but a whisper," he said, getting a beloved poem wrong, as usual, but also somehow actually getting it right this time.

Principal Barkin approached the glass case and peered at his father's trophy.

"Well that's very nice," said Principal Barkin, "but nobody ever looks in here."

"That's kind of the point," said Miles.

"It is?" said Principal Barkin.

"Grace notes," said Miles.

"A masterstroke," said Niles, "to our whole career."

"Hmm," said Principal Barkin. He thought about this for a while. "Hmm. But who will know this prank even happened?"

"Just me and Niles," said Miles.

"And also me!" said Principal Barkin. "Ha, ha! Well I like *that*."

Miles and Niles nodded.

"I guess this means it's really coming to an end, the end of an era, the Terrible Twos epoch."

"Terrible Two," said Miles.

"The Terrible Two epoch," said Principal Barkin. "I don't suppose you'd consider teaming up with some other prankster in Miles's absence, Niles, and including me in some of your capers. The Terrible Two 2! It could be you and Scotty!"

"I don't really know anything about Scotty," said Niles.

"Me neither," said Barkin. "It wouldn't even have to be pranks! You could solve mysteries!" Principal Barkin frowned. "Although it wouldn't be the same without Miles, would it?"

"No," Niles said.

206

"Ah! Miles! You could stay here! With me! I would raise you, sort of like my son! And I'd be sort of like your dad! Wow!"

"Um," said Miles. "Thanks."

"That feels really far-fetched, Principal Barkin," said Niles.

"It is," said Principal Barkin. "I know it is. I just don't want it to be over."

"Yeah," said Niles.

"Yeah," said Miles. "I'll miss you, Principal B."

"Oh!" said Principal Barkin. "Well! Well, well, well. Well. Thank you, Miles."

For a little bit, nobody talked.

Then Principal Barkin did.

"In case you boys are in the mood for one more jape, I was coming to ask if you wanted to sneak away from this dance and hang this picture up in my old man's office."

He turned the frame around so the boys could see the painting inside.

Miles and Niles laughed, which made Principal Barkin beam.

"Pretty good, eh?" he said, winking.

"Really good," said Niles.

"But you don't need to wink," said Miles.

"You know, I decided," said Principal Barkin, "I'm going to run against him this year! For superintendent!" Principal Barkin was swept away by visions of his campaign. The speeches! The coffee! Maybe there could even be some patriotic bunting! His gaze grew fuzzy as he imagined it all. "Is this a yard sign I see before me? With purple letters, all in caps! VOTE BARKIN! ME, BARRY BARKIN, THAT IS, AND NOT MY FATHER, BERTRAND!"

"Sounds like a big lawn sign," said Niles.

"It will be a huge lawn sign!" said Principal Barkin.

"I hope you win," said Miles.

"But you won't even be here!" said Principal Barkin.

"I know," said Miles. "But I still hope you win."

"Well that is very kind of you, Miles Murphy. Very kind indeed. Now let's go! The dance is ending soon and we have a portrait to hang!"

They were on their way to the exit when the doors to the gym opened and Holly poked her head through. The opening strains of a song leaked out into the hallway. It was a slow song.

"Last dance, kids!" said the DJ. "Last dance, yo!"

"Hey, everybody," said Holly. "Hey, Niles. Wanna dance?"

Miles looked at Niles.

Principal Barkin looked at Niles.

"Yeah," Niles said.

Holly led Niles to the middle of the dance floor, where they joined a clump of slowly swaying kids. Stuart was there, moving his arms like a puppeteer. Scotty and Janice Neeser were dancing together for something like the ninth time. Josh Barkin was over by a wall, doing karate moves to a tumbling mat.

Principal Barkin and Miles stood in the doorway, watching Niles.

"That's a good kid right there," said Principal Barkin.

"Yeah," said Miles.

Principal Barkin looked back at the trophy case. "A wonderful prank, Miles, from one prankster to another. Although my favorite prank of yours will always be your first prank, when you parked my car on the steps, which I still don't know how you did."

"I didn't."

"If you think about it," said Principal Barkin, "that trophy case is now a wonderful metaphor, and, as you know, I have a gift for metaphor. Because that trophy case is changed, but the change is something nobody will see. You, Miles, have left the case altered, invisibly, but irrevocably, forever. Or at least until this school is torn down. Which hopefully it never will be, unless we pass a bond measure and get to build a new, better school, which would be excellent. But still, you have made a beautiful, invisible change. That trophy is like a heart, in a rib cage. It is even like *my* heart in *my* rib cage, which, and maybe it is just this sad and lovely song we're hearing, but I want to tell you that you have changed me, Miles Murphy. And when

you change a person, that change is invisible, although it can also be visible, for instance my purple ties, which, of course, I know I have already mentioned. But you have changed my heart, Miles Murphy. You and Niles both, although I have always loved having Niles as a student, but you, well, I want to tell you now that I feel very glad you moved to Yawnee Valley, even for a short while. I have been very lucky to have you at my school, Miles Murphy, and you are also a good kid. A great kid."

"Thanks," said Miles. He looked up at his principal. "I thought you were too old to change."

"Well, as usual, Miles, you were wrong."

Miles smiled. They watched the students dance. Principal Barkin adjusted the painting under his arm, which was growing heavy and causing him some discomfort. "How long is this song anyway?"

(It was the album version, five minutes, forty-eight seconds, but that's not really important.)

S BATTLE
ENDENT RACE

Superintendent and longtime Principal of YVSLA, Bertrand Barkin.

Barkin of A
ifferent Stripe

ABOUT *the* AUTHORS

MAC BARNETT is a *New York Times* bestselling author of many books for children, including *Extra Yarn*, illustrated by Jon Klassen, which won a 2013 Caldecott Honor and the 2012 *Boston Globe–Horn Book* Award for Excellence in Picture Books; *Sam & Dave Dig a Hole*, also illustrated by Jon Klassen and a 2015 Caldecott Honor winner; and *Battle Bunny*, written with Jon Scieszka and illustrated by Matthew Myers. He also writes the Brixton Brothers series of mystery novels.

JORY JOHN is the author of the picture books *Goodnight Already!* (with Benji Davies) and *I Will Chomp You* (with Bob Shea) and coauthor of the national bestseller *All My Friends Are Dead*; a sequel, *All My Friends Are STILL Dead*; and *Pirate's Log: A Handbook for Aspiring Swashbucklers*, among other books. Jory spent six years as programs director at 826 Valencia, a nonprofit educational center in San Francisco.

KEVIN CORNELL is the illustrator of many children's books, including *Count the Monkeys* and *Mustache!*, both by Mac Barnett.

OTHER BOOKS IN THE SERIES

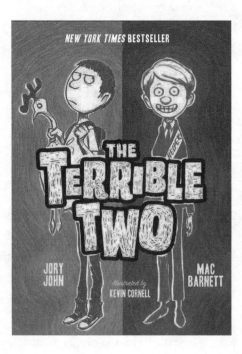

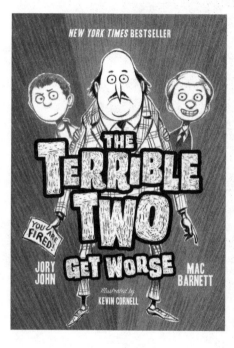

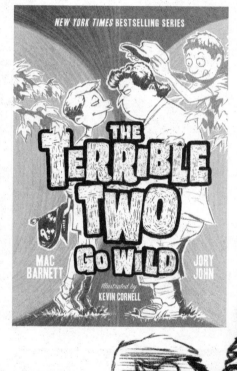

FOR KEV

Cataloging-in-Publication Data has been applied for and may be obtained from the Library of Congress.

ISBN 978-1-4197-2565-4

Text copyright © 2018 Mac Barnett and Jory John
Illustrations copyright © 2018 Kevin Cornell
Book design by Chad W. Beckerman

Printed and bound in U.S.A.
10 9 8 7 6 5 4 3 2 1

Amulet Books are available at special discounts when purchased in quantity for premiums and promotions as well as fundraising or educational use. Special editions can also be created to specification. For details, contact specialsales@abramsbooks.com or the address below.

Amulet Books® is a registered trademark of Harry N. Abrams, Inc.

ABRAMS The Art of Books
195 Broadway, New York, NY 10007
abramsbooks.com